No part of this publication may be reproduced, stored in a retrieval system, or transmitted in any form or by any means, electronic, mechanical, photocopying, recording, scanning, or otherwise, without the prior written permission of the publisher, except in the case of brief quotations within critical reviews and otherwise as permitted by copyright law.

NOTE: This is a work of fiction. Names, characters, places, and incidents are a product of the author's imagination. Any resemblance to real life is purely coincidental. All characters in this story are 18 or older.

Copyright © 2016, Willow Winters Publishing. All rights reserved.

Tommy
&
Tonya

Willow Winters
Wall street journal & usa today bestselling author

From USA Today bestselling author Willow Winters comes a HOT mafia, standalone romance.

I didn't plan on stumbling into Tommy, the muscle of the Valetti crime family.

He warns me to stay away,
but holds the key to everything I need.

All of this started because I wanted the truth.
I need answers to numb the pain of my past.
It was never supposed to be anything else.

He makes me beg when I've never pleaded
with anyone for a damn thing.
He makes me crave something I never imagined.
He makes me wish I could hold on to this moment and forget everything else.

He's a thug, a mistake, and everything I need...

Cuffed Kiss

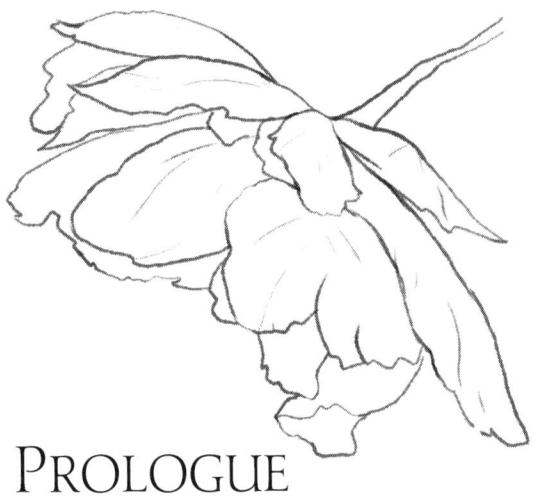

Prologue

Tommy

I push the cuffs together and grin when I hear them *click, click, click,* as they slowly tighten around her wrists. She's not going anywhere now.

Tonya

"Tommy, please," I plead with him. My pussy clenches as his hot breath tickles my neck, sending shivers down my body and making my nipples harden. I don't even know why I'm begging him. This is exactly what I wanted. He's what I need.

"I told you to stay away," I whisper into the crook of her neck. My hand travels slowly up her thigh, sending tremors down her body.

I rock my pussy into his hand as his fingers shove my

panties to the side. I shouldn't want this, but I do. And I fucking love it. He pushes his hand harder against my pussy, letting me take my pleasure from him. Even though my eyes are closed, I know he's smirking at me for giving in to him.

"You knew what I'd do to you if you came around, didn't you?" I ask her, even though I already know the answer.

"Yes," I whisper as his fingers gently circle my clit, sending a hot wave of pleasure through my body.

"You deliberately disobeyed me, didn't you?" I ask her as I slowly push two thick fingers into her welcoming heat. She arches her back and pulls against her restraints. She's so fucking wet. So ready for me.

I bite my bottom lip and muffle my moans of pleasure. He pulls his hand away, leaving me wanting, and my eyes pop open, already missing his touch. My body sags on the bed as I pant, waiting for him.

I'm the muscle of the *familia*, and under investigation. This shit isn't supposed to happen. But I want her. And I always get what I want.

I'm a cop. I shouldn't be fucking around with a thug like him. I should know better, but my body is begging for his touch. And I can't tell him no.

Just one more time, before I have to say goodbye.

Just one more time, before it all comes to an end.

"You're such a bad girl, aren't you?" I give her clit a light smack with the back of my hand before climbing off the bed to unzip my jeans, letting them fall to the floor.

"I'm your bad girl." My voice is barely above a murmur as he climbs between my legs. It hurts saying the words, because after today, I'll never see him again. I can't. But I want to be his bad girl.

That's right, she's mine. All fucking mine. At least right now she is.

I wish I could just stay here in this moment. I don't want this to end.

I slam my dick into her tight pussy all the way to the hilt, and stay deep inside her as her walls clench around me. She screams out and bucks against me, trying to get away, but all she needs is a moment to adjust. She feels so fucking good. Each time is better than the last. I'll never be able to fuck this broad out of my system.

My body tingles with an icy sensation as he pounds into me. Every nerve ending feels lit up, ready to spark, threatening to go off and consume me. The bed dips with each thrust and I instinctively pull against the cuffs, needing to touch him. The only sounds are the clinking of metal, our frantic breathing, and his hard thrusts.

Her heels dig into my ass, wanting more as I rut between her legs. My fingers dig into her hips to keep her still, to make her take it. She asked for this; she begged for this by coming to me again.

I tilt my hips as he pushes deeper inside of me. A strangled cry escapes my throat as he pushes me to the brink of pain, then leaves me wanting more. He pulls out almost all the way, teasing me, but gives me what I need before I have to beg for it.

My ears are filled with the sexy sounds of her moaning. She's so loud that she's almost drowning out the sounds of my dick slamming into her hot cunt. I fucking love it. It encourages me to fuck her harder. I never want to stop hearing her cries of pleasure.

He slams into me and groans, the sound lingering in the hot air between us. It's the sexiest sound I've ever heard. My body heats in waves, and the tips of my fingers and toes go numb. I'm so close. I moan and whimper, and stare into his dark eyes as my orgasm hits me with a force that renders my scream silent.

The sight of her cumming on my dick is my undoing. I press my body against hers and thrust with short, shallow

pumps, filling her until our combined cum leaks down and onto the sheets.

He kisses the crook of my neck, and I turn my head to eagerly take his lips with my own. My heart clenches in pain as I surrender all of my passion into our final kiss. Tears threaten to fall, but I push them away. I know this was our last time, but I don't want it to be over.

I keep my lips on hers as I reach up and unlock her cuffs with the key. As soon as one wrist is free, her hand's in my hair, pulling me closer to her.

I just need to feel him; I need to remember this. I don't want it to end. I wish I could live in this moment forever.

As I pull away, I see her eyes are closed and I know she wants this, too.

I wanna make her happy; I wanna keep my bad girl. And I will.

Everything and everyone else be damned. I can't say goodbye to her.

I'm not letting her go.

Chapter 1

Tommy
Three Weeks Earlier

I run my hand through my hair and take another look out of the window. Nothing yet. My apartment is a few stories up, but I can see down below to the first floor from here. I'm expecting a few cop cars to show up any minute now, sirens blaring. We got word a little earlier from the judge that he had to approve my arrest. He's in our pocket, but there's only so much even he can do.

They have enough to bring me in for questioning, so I just need to keep my mouth shut. And I can do that--I've had plenty of practice.

"Quit worrying," my brother says from the other side of the living room. I turn to face Anthony as he pours more whiskey into our glasses. The ice clinks softly against the glass as he hands me my drink before taking a sip from his. "At least this will give you something to do." He chuckles at his own joke.

"Yeah, I'm bored to fucking tears." I've been keeping a low profile, which means no family business. I don't know what the fuck to do with myself. I'm used to going out and getting shit done. Instead I'm holed up, waiting for this to be over. I miss being out there and making sure the Valettis are still respected and feared like we should be.

I'm the best of the best at keeping that fear alive. I'm six-foot-two, and muscle on top of muscle. I know some fucker is going to mess with our shit. They always do. And right now I can't do shit about it. Instead I'm sitting here on my ass, being a good little boy while the judge works his magic and Kane takes over my position.

"It's not like this is your first time." He smirks at me and I grunt a humorless laugh.

Anthony does the hits, and all the shit behind the scenes. He's never been taken in, not like the rest of us in the *familia*. Lucky fucker. When you work on the streets like I do, you get hauled in every once in awhile. Usually it doesn't faze me, but this is different. I'm not gonna lie, it'd be nice to get a gig like Anthony's and not have to deal with this shit.

The first time I was taken in was back when I was 22 years old. A low-life asshole thought he could steal from us. He was a fucking idiot. No one steals from us Valettis. We're well-known, feared, and respected. More so now than we were back then. But junkies will do whatever it takes to get their next hit. The poor bastard knew it was coming, too.

I found the fucker shooting up outside of a strip joint. He was in the back alley. Couldn't even wait till he got home, I guess. It doesn't bother me much now, but back then it took a toll on me. I hadn't toughened up yet. I broke his arm first. I learned that from my pop. Grab, twist, and crack. That way it's more difficult for them to fight back. He didn't even see me coming until his arm was busted and hanging limp at his side. I had to rough him up a bit. It was one of my first errands, and I knew the *familia* would go checking up behind me to see what kind of a job I'd done.

We agreed on new terms to the deal while he sat huddled in his own piss in that dark, filth-covered alley. And by that I mean he agreed to pay it all back with hefty interest by the next day. I have no clue if he ever paid up. I can't imagine if and how he did, but then again, that's not my job. And I don't ask questions.

Unfortunately, a little old lady saw us and decided to do the right thing. She stood at the entrance to the alley. I remember how her silhouette blocked the golden glow illuminating us from the street light. She was a small, frail woman in a cardigan, and had a plastic bag from the drugstore next door hanging from her wrist. When I looked her in the eyes, daring her to reach for her phone, she looked back with no fear at all. Feisty old woman.

I didn't bother dealing with her the way we normally handle witnesses. I figured the punk would live, but his ass wasn't going to press charges. That, and I'd only killed once before. That fucker had it coming to him, but this woman didn't. I wasn't getting her blood on my hands.

The prick ran out of the alley ahead of me and knocked her to the ground as she dialed the police. Having done my part, I took off and prayed she wouldn't be able to identify me. After all, it was dark, I was clad in all black, and I never got close enough to her so she could really see me. Or so I thought.

Old bat did see me though, and the cops knew exactly who she was describing. They know we're the mob, so they're always waiting for a chance to pin something on us. And I gave it to them, like a dumbfuck. Uncle Dante reamed me out pretty good. He was the Don back then, before his son Vince took over.

Luckily, nothing ever came of it. A night in the slammer, and I was a free man. That was the first time. Since then I've been careful, but occasionally we get pulled in for questioning. It's rare to spend a night in jail, though. Not when we have the best lawyer money can buy, and more than enough cops and judges on our payroll to make up our own court system. We always know when we'll be detained ahead of time, so we're always prepared.

But this time, fuck--this time it could be the real thing for me. The uncertainty surrounding this arrest is different from all the other times, and I don't like it.

"You're gonna be fine," Anthony says, taking a seat on my sofa. He drapes his arms across the back of the grey leather couch, and I wish I were as relaxed as him. I've never been envious of Anthony. He's a few inches shorter than me, and between the two of us, I'm the bigger pussy magnet. But right now I wish I'd been smart like him and and taken a job that didn't have me risking my neck like this.

"He said there's a good bit of evidence," I point out. Those are the words I keep hearing. *Good bit of evidence.*

"What are they gonna charge you with, huh?" He takes a swallow of his whiskey and leans forward, setting his drink down on the glassy surface of the coffee table before answering his own question. "Doing their job for 'em?" He says it sarcastically with a raised brow.

We got into a tight spot with some business partners, Abram Petrov and his crew. He was a big fucking deal, along with his supposed second-in-command Vadik Mikhailov. They took over international territories like it was nothing. Then he came here and wanted us to deal in the sex trafficking industry. That's not our thing. Unfortunately, when you tell people 'no' in our line of business, cutting ties takes on a whole new meaning.

"Murder, that one's legit," I finally respond. Thirteen

dead members of Petrov's crew were left at the scene, along with twelve women we made certain were safe in the back room. We had a heads-up from Kane about Petrov's plan to murder us, so Petrov and his crew went down easier since they didn't know our ambush was coming.

Now the cops are trying to pin it all on me. I was the one stupid enough to leave evidence behind. Usually the clean-up crew gets all of it. But this time, they didn't. It's not like I was sloppy--I'm never sloppy. Shit just falls through the cracks sometimes. And this time it might fuck me over real good.

"Stop sweating it. They're just trying to get something from you," Anthony points out, still trying to reassure me. I should listen to Anthony. My brother's got great intuition, and he's always right. "I'll be there to pick you up when you're done, waiting right outside." He picks up his drink again, taking another pull before continuing. "And I bet the ice in my drink won't even be melted by the time you're getting into my ride." He swirls the ice around in the glass for emphasis as he says it.

He keeps my gaze, but I have to break it. I have a sick feeling in my gut. Vince says it'll be fine, that the judge says some of the evidence is inadmissible. But *some* is not all, and something deep down is telling me they're going to get me this time. It was way too big of a scene to clean up. Too much shit on our turf. We've been laying low, but it's going to blow up in our faces. I just know it.

Tilting my head to the left and right, I crack my neck

on both sides. I down the remainder of my glass, savoring the sensation of the cold liquid mixed with the hot burn of the whiskey. It slides down my throat and warms my chest. That's when I hear them. I take a heavy breath and roll out my shoulders, knowing they'll be hurting once the cuffs are on. Gotta loosen them up now. Somehow, hearing the wail of the sirens get louder as they approach puts me at ease. Maybe it's just the waiting part that irritates me.

My heartbeat steadies, and my nerves follow suit. It's just like any other day, I tell myself. I'm used to this. These high-stress situations can't faze me. I can't let them see me in any other states but calm and confident. No one ever gets to see me in any other condition than prepared. If they view you otherwise, you give them a chance to think of you as weak. And that's one thing I'm not.

"That's the brother I know." Anthony gets up and walks past me to the window, tipping the upper blinds back to get a better view. "Oh, five," he says as his voice rises sarcastically. "You're so fucking special." I chuckle and pat him on the back as I head to the door.

Him being so at ease and having a sense of humor about it all does help. I gotta admit, whenever I'm in this shit, he's always here for me, before and after. The other guys are at the bar, but I know they'll be waiting for me there when I get out, too. That's something the *familia* is always good for, buying you a drink when you get out.

"You're not gonna make them walk their asses all the way up here? Seems like a missed opportunity to me." He shakes his head with a grin.

"You just wanna watch, don't you?" I ask him with a smirk.

He pats my back again and sets his glass down on the end table. "I'll go with you."

I grin at him as I open the door and hear the sounds of them walking through the building. I decide to leave my apartment unlocked. I know they're going to search my place, and I'd rather not have to replace my door in case they decide to be assholes. "Lock it up for me when they're gone?"

Anthony nods. "You know I will." They're already climbing the stairs as we get to the landing, so I just stand there with my hands clearly visible. I don't want these fuckers to shoot my ass.

"It's all good, Tommy. Just remember that. Not a damn thing's gonna happen," he says under his breath with a straight face. His smiles and jokes are all gone. He's doing the same thing as me and putting on his mask.

I'm large and all muscle. I look like I'd fuck you up with my bare hands, and you'd be right to think that. Anthony has a different air around him, he always has. He's a little shorter than me, a lot leaner, but toned. But something about his expressions and his dark eyes lets you know not to fuck with him.

"Thomas Valetti, we have a warr--" the cop closest to me begins, as he starts pulling out a piece of paper, but I don't even need to see it.

I cut him off and don't let him finish. "Yeah yeah, I know." I turn and put my hands on the top of my head.

As a set of hands grab my wrists to pull them behind my back, and a voice starts spouting off the standard bullshit, I look up and see Anthony.

I almost don't see it, but I know I do. I see a flash of worry in Anthony's eyes. And that's the only thing that keeps playing through my head as they take me in.

Chapter 2

Tonya

I'm fucking furious. It feels like I'm back in high school again, dealing with petty, catty drama. I didn't like it then, and I don't like it now. The only difference is that I can't meet up behind the school to put this bitch in his place. I may be small, but I could take him. It wouldn't be the first time I've had to prove myself.

"This is bullshit, Harrison, and you know it!" I slam the folder down on my desk and push off my chair so fast it almost tips over. I don't give a shit. I also don't give one fuck that my skirt is all wrinkled and riding up from sitting at my desk all day. If it was up to me, I wouldn't be sitting at this damn desk. I'm not a paper pusher; I like getting shit done, and I hate that he's trying to stand in my way.

"Is there a problem, Officer Kelly?" he asks me with a twisted smile. He's such an ass. He went behind my back to have more paperwork assigned to me. If he thinks he can wear me down until I'm his little bitch, he has another think coming. I'm a fighter. That's what I do, and I'm damn good at it.

"Oh, now I'm 'Officer Kelly'?" This angry woman, yelling at her coworker? This isn't me. But I'm so pissed. I hate my temper, and I've worked so fucking hard to tone it down. I really hate getting angry. But Harrison brings out the worst in me.

I'm fed up with this asshole. He's a crooked cop, and now he's trying to boss me around. I might be new, but I want to be the lead on this case more than anything. It's the only reason I'm here, and I won't let him stand in my way. Motherfucker better back off. I don't care that he has more experience than me; what he's doing is wrong.

"Thomas Valetti is a criminal," he says from the doorframe of my office. There's conviction in his voice. I get that. I know Thomas is mobbed up; everyone knows the Valettis are the big time mafia around here. But that doesn't mean he should be going down for this.

"He didn't do this, and you know it." My voice wavers, and I hate that it does. I wish it were steady and strong. I *am* strong, but I feel like I'm on the verge of breaking.

"You don't know shit." I swear I see spit fly from his mouth as he sneers his words. "If you knew what I had to deal with from these lowlifes, you'd be chomping at the bit to get him in here and sweating in his seat." *'Lowlifes'* hits a nerve with me. I've been called a lowlife before more than once. I grew up in a trailer until my mom got clean. It wasn't my fault. If I'd had a choice, I wouldn't have lived there. I wanted real walls around my bedroom, not thin sheets of metal that barely protected me from anything that happened to bang against them in the middle of the night.

My only saving grace was my sister. I'll never understand how we grew up in the same environment, yet turned out so different. After we moved to the suburbs, she just naturally fit in. It didn't take long for me to settle down and find ways to fit in as well, but I never forgot who I was. She was a good girl through and through. It's not that I was a bad girl. I just had to tame that spitfire in me and throw my favorite sparkly pink polish on top so I could blend in better.

He walks closer to me with a scowl on his face. "He's one of the big fish in the family. We can get him to talk. I know we can."

That's what this is about. He's looking for anything he can get to put the Valettis behind bars. But not this way. I fucking hate that he's chasing a name and bending the law. What's right is right, and what's wrong is wrong. And right now what Detective Harrison is doing is just plain wrong.

I learned long ago that if you just do what's right, bad shit tends to stay away from you. Most of the time. My heart clenches in my chest and I almost reach for the locket I used to wear every day, but I don't. Sometimes bad shit just happens, but you still try to do the right thing.

Harrison and his vendetta could fuck this up for me. I don't care about past crimes. Shit, I don't even care about whatever the hell the Valettis are doing now. I care about one name, and getting the information I need to make sure he pays. I care about revenge.

Some may think it's wrong, taking revenge. But it's not. Not for me. My sister deserves justice, and I won't stop until she gets it.

I speak through clenched teeth, arching my neck to look this prick in his eyes. He might be taller than me, but he's not going to intimidate me. At least not so much that it's completely obvious to him. "You and I both know Petrov had that deal lined up with the Bratva in Kirov." All the wire transfers and cell phone activity point to it. He knows it, and I know it. It's fucking obvious, and international relations corroborated our theory. The Valettis put an end to that shit, and got a target on their backs for their troubles. Yet Detective Harrison is ready to pin the entire case on Thomas Valetti. The evidence is weak at best, but he's pushing.

"You'll stick to the script, or spend every fucking day sifting through these files, Kelly."

"I'm not your goddamned secretary." I walk past him and head straight to the Lieutenant's office. I'm done with this conversation. Since I can't kick his ass, I'll just go around him. He's not my boss, and I'm not going to put up with this.

I knock on the closed door with my white-knuckled fist and keep my back to Harrison as he stomps up behind me. His shadow looms over me. I can't fucking stand him. He crosses the line whenever the hell he wants. I'm tired of him ordering me around and threatening me when he's the one in the wrong. I know I'm new and I have to prove myself, but there comes a point when it's just him being an asshole.

I raise my fist to pound against the door again, but it flies open.

"Harrison!" Jerry Weldon is an old man who's tired of Harrison's shit, too. I have to work hard to keep the grin from showing on my face.

"Lieutenant--" Harrison tries to speak over me, but Jerry cuts him off.

"I swear to God, if this is over the Valetti case, I'm going to fucking pull you off it, Harrison." The grin slips into place, and I feel like a damn villain for enjoying this. But I can't help it.

"He's threatening to take me off, Lieutenant," I say as calmly and professionally as possible. Which is easier than I'd thought it'd be. I can play the good girl part when I have to.

Jerry's eyebrow cocks and he looks at Harrison like the fucking cockroach he is, then back at me. "I don't have time for this shit, Kelly. Ignore his ass for now and do your damn job." The blood drains from my face. Fuck. I hate that he's scolding me like a petulant child. I just want Harrison off my ass. Is that too much to ask?

Again I feel like I'm in high school. The teachers looked at me with sympathy because they thought I just couldn't help that I was always getting into trouble. It was bullshit then, and it's bullshit now. I swear to God some days I feel like I've taken crazy pills.

"He's in holding now, and you'll interview him together. Is that clear?" Jerry asks, looking between both of us.

"Yes, sir." I answer clearly while Harrison practically mumbles. I didn't bust my ass to get here so that I'd have to stand by men like him. He earned this position, and I should respect him for it. I *try* so hard to respect him for it. If he'd stop being an asshole, it'd be easier. I know the Valettis are big fish, but this is *my* case. And he needs to stop trying to shut me out of it.

I would cave and drop it if it weren't for Petrov. He's the only reason I'm here, and if Harrison knew why, he'd stop trying to push me off the case, because he'd know there's no way I'm ever backing down. But none of them know; I don't want them to. I can't let them know this is personal.

Jerry gives me a tight smile, and I can see a faint glimmer of sympathy in his eyes. I'm not sure if it's because I'm standing next to this asshole and I don't have a choice, or if it's because he thinks I won't make it.

I'm petite, I like the color pink, especially *hot* pink, and

I'd rather smile and joke around than brood over something stupid. Or I used to, anyway. Now it seems like all I do is get pissed off. But that's an exception. It's because I'm forced to deal with an ass all day.

All of those girly touches I love so much make me seem young and naive. Everyone looks at me like I don't belong, and maybe they're right. Maybe I learned to like all of that girly stuff because it softened me up some. Maybe I just wanted to copy my sweet-as-sugar sister. I don't know. I'm a tough girl, but I'm still a girl. I don't understand why people don't think I can be both, like they're mutually exclusive or something. Instead I'm judged and shunned, no matter how many times I prove I have what it takes.

I stopped wearing anything remotely fashionable to the social gatherings. Even though I have palettes upon palettes of eyeshadow, I keep my makeup simple, or I just don't wear makeup at all. I don't wear any jewelry or get my nails done anymore. I have to wear my hair up in a ponytail or a bun. When it's down I look way too feminine. I do everything I can to look like I fit in, because apparently that's a requirement here. It doesn't matter that I graduated at the top of my class back at the academy. A girly girl can't survive here. Or so they say behind my back.

The problem is that they don't see my confidence and passion for what it is. My personality's misconstrued because of how I look. I'm a bad ass bitch when I need to be, but I don't want to come off that way all the time. I haven't proven myself to be strong in their eyes.

I'm pushing the bad bitch to the surface and repressing every other part of me. All that's left after getting rid of the frilly shit I love is just a tough girl trying to fit in, so I can do what I came here to do. But I'm failing, and that fucking sucks, because I don't fail at anything, and this is the only thing that matters anymore. I have to work twice as hard, to be considered half as good.

When I hear the guys talking shit about being tough, all I can think is that they're talking about tough actions, not appearances or words. Maybe they're just trying to convince themselves that a petite woman with a penchant for pink couldn't kick their asses. I'm happy to prove them wrong though.

A part of me wants to prove them wrong. I want to show them I'm a bad ass bitch when I need to be. But another part of me is tired of fighting their prejudice. I didn't come here to win their approval. They can talk shit about me. They can assume I'm going to fail. I don't give a fuck. All I need is to be on this case. It's the only reason I put up with this shit.

It hurts though. I'm woman enough to admit it. I want companionship. I want to feel like I belong. But right now, I have no one. I try to call my mom every once in awhile, but that's just depressing as hell. I'm most concerned with the fact that I don't know what happiness is anymore. I don't know what I expected. But this isn't it. I was so shortsighted with wanting to get here that I didn't think things through all the way.

The reality is a swift kick in the ass.

Harrison pushes past me just as I get to the door to the interrogation room. Fucker holds it open for me though, like he's a gentleman. I give him a tight smile and walk in first.

I almost stop when I see the hulking man in the metal chair. An air of power surrounds him. His hands are clasped in front of him and they're resting on the table. He doesn't bother to look up at us. His dark, thick hair is longer on top than it is on the sides, just long enough to grip onto. It tempts me; it excites the wilder side of me that I usually keep suppressed.

He's in a simple white t-shirt that stretches tight over his shoulders, and faded blue jeans. I've never seen a man who could make those casual clothes look so fucking hot. His arms are all thick, corded muscle, and they flex as Harrison walks in front of me and stands across from him. Dark tattoos scroll down his left arm. I find myself itching to touch them, and wonder how much of his body they cover.

The younger me would have drooled over this man, but I know better now. Men like him cause more trouble than they're worth. And he's a member of the strongest *familia* on this side of the country. He's a Valetti. He's trouble.

"Valetti." Harrison's nose scrunches as he sits in the seat across from the sexy-as-fuck suspect. I stand with my back against the wall. I don't want to go near those two knowing what Harrison is up to. I'm not afraid to get into it if I have to. I can hold my own, regardless of how big and how scary my opponent is. But I'm not fucking stupid. I avoid physical altercations if I can. And Harrison has a smart mouth and likes to push people.

He likes to take advantage of these situations and get them to act out so he can put them in the cells and threaten a heavier sentence. It's not a move I'd make. But I try not to judge other officers' tactics. I *try*. Never said I was perfect though.

The man, Thomas Valetti, raises his head slowly. His full lips tip into a slight smirk and his blue eyes hold a hint of humor. "Detective. Nice to see you again."

His voice sends a throbbing need to my clit, and for the first time since I've taken this job, I question if I really am cut out for it. I've never once been attracted to the fucked-up criminals that come and go in here. But right now, right here? Fuck. He's hot. My body can't deny that. I have to work really hard to keep the embarrassment off my face. I'm a professional. I'm a cop now. I need to put my hormones in check.

I try to ignore the pulsing need between my thighs and I clear my throat to help settle myself.

The action causes both men to look at me. Thomas' eyes roam my body, but not in a way I find rude or offensive. He's just sizing me up. I half-expect him to make some sexist comment, like most thugs do. I can *feel* my defenses go up.

His eyes reach mine and I wait for it. I wait for the dismissal. The demeaning comments I'm constantly used to getting.

Instead Harrison interrupts, "I won't stop until you go away for life."

The corners of Thomas' lips kick up slightly as he turns to face Harrison, leaving me with nothing. "Sorry, Detective. I'm just waiting for my lawyer."

Harrison looks at me from the corner of his eyes like it's my fault that Thomas isn't talking. I grab the folder from the desk and move to sit in the seat next to Harrison and square my shoulders.

I know in the pit of my gut Thomas Valetti is one of the people who saved those women. But he also has information I want. Now's my chance to make everything I've worked for up to this moment worth it.

He's my only lead.

Chapter 3

Tommy

"Mr. Valetti," begins the gorgeous woman who's all curves and sweetness. She's looking back at me like we're on good terms. Like she can talk to me as though I'm an old pal of hers. She's either fresh blood, or she's damn good at what she does. This good cop/bad cop routine would be easy enough with detective Harrison being the jackass he is. It's not the first time I've run into him, and I'm sure it won't be the last.

Judging by her body language when she walked in here, and the pissed-off looks Harrison keeps throwing her, I'm guessing she's new. I wouldn't mind having her try to cuff me. Wish it was her who'd brought me in, not that fuckface from earlier.

"We know you were at the scene of the crime *after* it

occurred based on the fact that your prints were found covering the prints of Lucas Mikhailov, a man found dead on sight." She reaches into the manila folder and slides a photograph of a doorknob across the table. Her small hand holds it in place. She doesn't move it, and I find myself eyeing her chipped nail polish. It's a soft cream color and it makes her appear even more dainty that she already looks. What the hell is this little thing doing trying to play cop? She interrupts my thought as she takes her hand away and asks, "Would you like to explain how that could've happened?"

I meet her gaze and love that she's not intimidated by me. Her eyes are the most beautiful shade of green I've ever seen. And they're staring back at me waiting for an answer. I'm real fucking sorry to disappoint her. But even a sweetheart like her can't get me to talk. I'm not saying shit.

I almost apologize--almost call her love, or sweetie. But I keep my mouth shut and remind myself that this is an act. These cops like to set the scene. It's all lies in here. I give her a simple shake of my head and answer, "I'm just waiting for my lawyer."

If I'm being honest with myself, this is the most nervous I've ever been, but I don't show it. I don't give them anything.

They have my prints, even though they're smudged, and so are the ones beneath mine. They have the tire tracks to the Escalade, which is in my name. They have a witness who says she saw me, although she was drugged up. At least that's the evidence the judge was willing to hand off to Vince. Three pieces of shit evidence. One piece of evidence by itself could be a coincidence. But put three pieces together, and it starts sounding real fucking bad.

"Mr. Valetti. Are you aware that a Miss Georgia Stevens was found dead in the back of the rental car left at the scene of the crime?" the sweet little thing in front of me says, and it takes me a moment to register what she said.

My heart skips a beat, and my blood goes cold. A dead woman. No. We saved those women. But we didn't check any cars. Fuck! I wanna ask whose car. I wanna know how she died. More importantly, was she alive when we left?

My eyes search hers. She could be lying. She could be fucking with me just to get me to talk. But I see her expression soften with compassion. She can tell I didn't know. I lean back in my seat and do my best to wipe every emotion off my face. It's quiet for a moment. It's been about an hour, so my lawyer should be here soon. I just need to hold on till then, and then I can look up the woman they found dead. Vince never said shit about her. At least not to me, but I've been out of the loop.

"The car was rented to a man we believe to be Abram Petrov. His prints were found in the car, although his body was never found."

None of this is throwing up red flags to me. His body was sent back to the buyers as a sign from us that we weren't willing to partake in that aspect of the business. Our hands won't be forced. If they didn't know it then, well they sure as fuck know it now.

"Do you have any information regarding Petrov's whereabouts?" She leans forward, and I have to resist looking straight down her blouse. Her body is lean and toned with a touch of color from the sun, but her tits are bigger than you'd think they'd be for a woman as athletic as her.

I give her a weak smile and shake my head no again. I'm grateful for the bit of information she's given me, if it's true, but that doesn't mean I'm gonna talk. I need to know if the woman she mentioned was alive when we left. It couldn't have been more than twenty minutes before the cops got there. But a lot can happen in twenty minutes.

As if reading my mind, she answers my unspoken question. "Drug overdose," she says simply. My lips press into a tight line and my heart sinks. Maybe if my brother had seen her, like the other women, maybe he could've saved her. I drop my gaze to the edge of the table as I try to keep calm and not give her anything.

"She'd been dead for almost a day, judging by the autopsy." My eyes fly to hers. Thank fuck. That makes me feel better. I feel like an asshole for feeling any kind of relief. That poor woman didn't deserve to die, but at least she didn't die on our watch. We never had the opportunity to save her.

I run a hand through my hair and look at the closed door.

"Do you have any details that could help us uncover who was responsible?" I hear her sweet voice and I almost turn to her to answer, but I can't. We don't say shit except for what I've already given them. *I'm waiting on my lawyer.* That's the *familia* way.

"You don't have any fucking sympathy, do you?" Harrison starts up again with his shit from across the table. "The jury's gonna eat you alive." I resist rolling my eyes and sigh instead. This is fucking draining. Usually I don't give a fuck, but I am a bit worried. I don't like the sick feeling in my gut that keeps rising up on me.

"Are you charging me? If not, I'm gonna go ahead and leave," I say, looking at the door. I'm tired of waiting. I just want to get the hell out of here.

Harrison shoots up from his seat. I know he's coming over to get in my face. I stand up as he walks around the table. They can keep me here longer for questioning. I know that. But he's fucking lost it if he thinks he's gonna yell standing over me while I'm sitting down. That shit's not gonna fly.

I stand up and stare back at his narrowed eyes. I vaguely sense that the cute ass broad got up from her seat and is backing away. That puts me at ease. She doesn't need to get into this. She can keep playing the good cop part and stay the fuck out of the bad cop shit.

Harrison's body bumps into mine slightly, but I allow it. I know he's pushing me. He's done it before. Sometimes I get a little hotheaded. More than I should. But when you're here, in this position, you keep your cool. Otherwise you're just giving them a reason to keep you locked up. And that's the last thing I want.

"I'll charge you with everything possible, to the full extent of the law. Your ass isn't leaving here tonight. Or tomorrow. Or the next day." I focus my eyes on his crooked smile and imagine my fist slamming into it over and over. "Your big shot lawyer isn't getting you out of this one, Valetti."

His hands knock into my chest, palms first and push me backward ever so slightly. I'm a big fucker, and that's a bold fucking move for this little prick. I make a white-knuckled fist with my hand and clench my teeth.

Before I can even think about swinging, I feel the softest touch on my forearm. Gentle, but firm. And then it's gone. I don't turn to face her; I don't make any move that I even registered her touch. Harrison's yelling in my face, but my anger is gone and instead I find myself angling my body to guard her from this prick.

Why? No fucking clue. She's one of them. But I know she's just to my right. I can sense her there, and I don't like it.

She's a cop, and as far as I know she could hold her own. But I don't want her to. I track her to my right, hoping she doesn't try to get in between us. It might be sexist, but that's no place for a woman to be.

Harrison still hasn't caught on to the fact that him screaming in my face and subtly pushing his body against me isn't affecting me.

The sound of the door opening has Harrison taking a step back and trying to maintain eye contact with me, but I break it to watch her leave. He's no threat to me, so I couldn't give two shits about keeping an eye on him. But it wasn't her opening the door. Instead, my lawyer's standing in the doorway.

"Is there a problem here, Mr. Valetti?" Scott Kemmer is the *familia* attorney, and he's good at what he does.

I give him a tight smile and shove my hands into my pockets. "Not at all. I was just asking if it was time to go." I look over my shoulder and see the pretty little thing who didn't even bother to give me her name. Her eyes are shooting daggers at Harrison. I don't waste my energy to see what he's doing behind me. I bet she thought she could get me to talk if he wasn't being a prick and doing the shit he does.

She has no idea what she's up against, though. She'd never get an ounce of information from me. She must be *really* fucking new to think she'd get anything from a Valetti.

"Are you ready, Mr. Valetti?" I barely hear the words from my lawyer and that's when I belatedly realize I'm good to go. I didn't hear all the bullshit coming from Harrison about how I can't leave, and my lawyer's response. It's the same shit every time.

"All set." I give him a nod and make my way through the doors, not giving either one of them another look. But I have to admit, I wanna turn back and see her. I at least wanna know her name.

I let myself breathe freely for the first time all day as I leave the station, and see my brother in his car waiting for me, just like he said he would.

"Told you," Anthony says, lowering his window and giving our lawyer a salute.

"Hey, you wanna do something today?" I ask him.

Wicked curiosity flashes in his eyes.

"I wanna look someone up." He tilts his head and keeps his eyes on me as I round the car and get into the passenger seat.

"Look someone up?" he asks as I shut the door and lean back, making myself comfortable.

"Yeah, a cop," I tell him. The humor's completely wiped from his face until I add, "I think she's new."

"Oh, I see." He chuckles as he puts the car in drive. "Maybe we should've left you in there a little longer."

I laugh and roll my window down so I can put a hand out and feel the breeze.

"I'm just a little bored, and a lot curious," I say.

"You know what they say about that, don't you?" He looks at me like what I'm doing is stupid as fuck. And maybe it is. But I at least need to know her name.

Chapter 4

Tonya

I feel like a fucking failure. I sigh heavily and lean my back against the wall of the station. I run my hands over my face and feel like shit. Damn it's been a long couple of days. I got the approval to keep an eye on Thomas, so there's one positive thing that happened. Tomorrow I'll get something, even if it's just learning his routines. I have the next three days off. I can use them to get a good look at the Valettis and try to talk to Thomas. I may be off-duty, but if anything happens, I'll just say it's field work.

I really think I could've gotten information from him. I could tell he didn't have shit to do with Georgia's death. I could've fed off that emotion. I'm good at reading people, real fucking good at it. I get people to talk. There's just something about me that puts people at ease. I don't know what it is, but I love it. It's a gift, and it's always worked in my favor.

If Harrison had just shut his fucking mouth, I know I would've had Thomas right where I wanted him. I recognize the way he looked at me. I know what he was thinking. If I'd just kept it up, I would've had him talking to me and confiding in the poor, sweet girl who just wants to make things right. In some ways I'm a bitch for thinking that way. After all, I can be sweet. I just needed him to give me anything at all on Petrov. Everyone keeps saying he's probably dead. I need to know for sure.

If he's already dead and gone, it would kill the sick, twisted part of me that wants to beat him to death with my own two hands. I've spent years trying to find a way to get to him. I've come too close to give up hope. If he's dead, I *need* to know. I need to be able to let go. I can't really say goodbye to her until I know for sure.

The thought makes my eyes water, but I just blink a few times to shut that shit down. She would tell me not to cry, and if there's one person I took advice from, it was my sister. My fingers reach for my locket, the one with Melissa's picture in it. But it's not there, so instead I rub the dip in my throat. I never wear it when I'm on duty, but it does wonders to calm me down and keep me focused.

I shake my head to get rid of all the emotions threatening to consume me, and hit the unlock button on my key fob. The key itself is sticking out through my clenched fist. Just in case, I look to the right as the lights go off on my car and the gentle beep fills the air. I pass the corner of the building. No one's there. No one's out here. You can never be too careful, though. I always check. I'm always on guard. I'd say it comes with the training, but that's not why I do this. I wish I could lie to myself, but I can't. I know why I do it. And I hate the reminder.

I feel like I've felt eyes on me the last few days. So I guess being on guard like this may eventually pay off. I just can't get rid of the feeling that I'm being watched. My stomach coils into knots, and I try to shake it off. I'm just paranoid and tired. That's what I tell myself, over and over. This isn't the first time I've felt like this. And I was fine then. It's just my past that's haunting me.

I climb into my car and toss the messenger bag onto the passenger seat. I have so much paperwork to go through. I'm not looking forward to it, but if I have to work overtime to get it done and still be able to keep up with the Valetti case, then that's what I'm going to do.

I put the key in the ignition and start the car. My mind drifts as I drive back to my apartment. My sister was the only person I really had in this world. She was no one special to anyone but me. Just a nurse. No one who anyone would ever want to hurt. She never really went anywhere high-risk. She hardly went out for a drink. But one night she went out to get groceries and never came back. One night is all it took, and she was gone. Her body was found a few months later, among others, in Russia. At first I was filled with disbelief. This sort of thing doesn't happen in real life. Definitely not in America.

But it does. And it did to her. When I got over the sadness, the anger set in. I had nothing to hold me back. I was already in college for forensics, so it was a small step to get into the academy. Anger turned into determination. I read everything I could. I became obsessed.

It was almost like a graduation present that there was a position available in a town where Petrov was last seen in the US. I've never been so lucky. But since I've gotten here, the leads have gone cold. And so has everyone else I've been surrounded by.

I watch the red light as I pull up to it, waiting for it to turn green, and my eyes catch movement to my right. It's a small Italian water ice shop. A few kids are standing out front with their parents leaning into the window to order. I hear their little screams of joy as they each dig into their treats.

Their life is normal; I wonder if they do that every Friday night. We used to go to the ice cream parlor a few blocks away when we were younger. Melissa talked about how she would keep up the tradition with her kids when she bought her house close to where we grew up.

The light turns green and I slowly move along. I'll never have that again. I don't see how I can ever have a normal life. How can life go on when you've suffered that type of tragedy?

My mother's doped up on antidepressants. I'm surprised she didn't go back to coke. She's barely a shell of a human being. My father took off when I was young, so I don't even know him. So now I'm just ... alone. Chasing what may be a ghost. But I won't stop looking until I know for sure.

I pull into my spot and put the car in park. The street light is shining down perfectly, and the entrance to my building is only a few feet away. I make a quick exit and enter the building and only breathe once I've made it upstairs. I can't help that I feel this way. It's late, it's dark. Nothing good happens at this time of night.

I climb the stairs and make my way to my place. I take a look out of the peephole and expect to see someone watching, but I don't. There's no one there. I wish this paranoia would leave me. It's only been this bad for a few days, ever since I saw Thomas. The reminder brings me back to my sole purpose.

I lock the front door and walk calmly to my bedroom. The necklace is on my dresser. I pick it up and open the little oval locket.

I want to end this for her.

I have a feeling in my gut that Thomas Valetti is the next step. I always follow my intuition, and it's clearly pushing me to talk to him. I feel like I already know the truth, but I just need to hear him say it.

If I can just get an in with Thomas, I know he'll lead me to something.

Chapter 5

Tommy

"I mean, what's the worst they can do?" The Bratva may be pissed we took a shipment from them, but they should've known better than to assume Petrov could speak on our behalf. Apparently they *did* make that assumption though, and now they're saying we owe them. I lean back a bit on the bar stool and look around. We're in the bistro now, just chatting it up.

"They could come here, but I doubt they will. Too much effort," Kane says. Most of the guys are here, bullshitting and having a drink. I like Kane. He's new to the *familia*, but he knows his shit and he's good at what he does. Which right now is taking over my position.

"It's not the loss of one shipment, it's their entire trade structure that they have to rebuild. A few million in revenue," Vince says from across the bar. I cross my arms and take it in. They haven't threatened us, but they made it clear they were pissed.

"It's not our fault they were doing all their shit through Petrov," Joey says.

"Maybe sending his body to them instead of the women wasn't the way to go?" Anthony's question has a few of the men chuckling.

"I'm not sure it's even worth replying. It's not like we do business with these people." I offer up my opinion. We keep our trades to Mexico, and that's it. The new dealer there is low-key and reasonable. Nice and easy. None of this overseas shit.

"We need to respond with something." Vince takes another drink and adds, "I want this to be a clean break away from them, but I sure as shit am not buying them off." They want 2 million for their hardship, which is bullshit, and I know Vince isn't going to pay them. It's quiet for a few minutes.

"Fuck 'em," he finally says, "let 'em come to us. Tony's got eyes on their contacts here. We'll know they're coming before they strike." He puts his glass down and pulls out his phone. I know he's checking on his wife, Elle, and his little one. Angelo is a cutie and almost six months old now. Ever since he's made his arrival, Vince checks his phone on the hour every hour.

Marcus comes up behind me and pats my shoulder as he says, "Your shadow's out front." He says it loud enough so that the rest of the guys can hear. Anthony chuckles into his drink, "Funny how you wanted to keep an eye on her, and now she's coming to you." He smirks and throws back his drink.

I spent a couple days just watching her after I looked her up. I had Tony do a little digging, too. I can't shake this broad. She looks on edge every time she's alone, yet she's completely confident and at ease any other time. Something's off about her, and I wanna know what it is. She knows her shit though. She's a tough bitch, not quite the quiet, demure type I pegged her for. And she fucking hates Harrison. The first time I saw her mimicking him behind his back and rolling her eyes, I laughed so fucking hard I thought they were going to hear me. I like that about her, but there's something else there, too. Something that had me chasing her ass.

I'd be a fucking liar if I said something about fucking a cop doesn't have me interested. Most of the time I was watching her that's all I could think about Bending her ass over and taming that wild side of her. The taboo aspect has me getting hard thinking about using her own cuffs to chain her to my bed. I think I just need to fuck this broad out of my system.

Vince rolls his eyes and says, "You need to tell her to back the fuck off, Tommy. We have restraining orders for a fucking reason."

"We don't have them on her." I can hear how defensive

I am, and it throws Vince off. I'm quick to add, "I'm being watched and on lockdown; better her than that prick."

I like her watching me. I like knowing she's close. And besides, I'm inactive until I'm completely in the clear, so there's nothing to worry about there. If nothing else, it's giving me something else to take my mind off this shit.

"Well, get her out of here," Anthony says as he looks me up and down. "And try to keep your dick in your pants." The guys laugh as I stand up.

"I hear you." I'm ready to get out of here anyway.

Vince follows me to the door.

"I don't like this talk about fucking a cop," he says.

"I'm not, so it's all good." He watches me as I look past him at the door. I don't tell him I want to, but I'm too fucking obvious.

"You're a shit liar, Tommy."

"I'm not lying." I don't even believe me as I say it. But it's the truth. I haven't touched her. Yet.

"You're not telling the truth, either."

I open my mouth to respond, but I don't. He knows I wanna fuck her. Everybody fucking knows it.

"You're looking for trouble, Tommy," Vince says in a lowered voice. "And that's what you're going to get."

"I'm not gonna do anything stupid, boss." He's gotta know I wouldn't say shit to her. I'd never breathe a word of anything.

"Women make us do stupid shit. And she's a cop." He stares

into my eyes, willing me to listen to him. "Don't fucking believe a word she tells you." His hand grips my shoulder as I nod.

I know this shit looks bad. I don't know why I'm drawn to this broad. She could fuck me over in a heartbeat. I'm not going to give her shit. But the thought of playing with her is giving me a high I haven't felt before. I know she wants in, and I'm dying to find out how much I can push her.

Vince shakes his head as he warns me, "Do not fuck this up to get your dick wet."

"I won't say shit, Vince. You know I won't risk the *familia*."

He huffs a laugh and pinches the bridge of his nose. "I'm not worried about that shit, I'm worried about you fucking a cop, Tommy. Tell me you aren't trying to get into her pants and I'll feel better."

I hesitate to answer. I'm not gonna lie. I wanna fuck this broad, she's hot as shit and the idea of those lips wrapped around my cock has my dick hardening every fucking time it comes to mind. Even right fucking now.

"Jesus, Tommy," he says with exasperation. Fuck. I don't wanna piss off the Don.

"I won't," I say with regret in the pit of my stomach.

"You're fucking lying to me," he says, although he doesn't sound that pissed about it.

"I've never lied to you before." I look him in the eyes, "if you're telling me to stay away from her, I'll end this shit right now and threaten a restraining order."

"Good. End this shit," he says with relief and finality in his voice. Well that fucking sucks. I take a frustrated breath and leave the guys to go tell her she needs to stay away.

I feel a wave of disappointment as I leave the bistro. But then I see her walking toward me with quick steps. She's in civilian clothes. Jeans that hug her curves and a teal tank top that rides up a little as she walks. The color brings out her eyes.

I can play a little more. Just a little before I have to give her up.

Fuck, no. I told Vince I wouldn't, and I know I shouldn't.

I hate that I want her and that I can't go after her. But I have to listen to Vince.

Chapter 6

Tonya

"Thomas." I call out his name as he blatantly turns away from me and starts heading down the street. I know he saw me. He fucking smiled before blowing me off.

I have to jog to catch up to him, but before I can put my hand on his shoulder to stop him, he turns around.

"What the hell are you thinking, Tonya?" he asks with more concern in his voice than anything else. "You could get yourself into serious shit hanging around out here waiting for me."

My brow furrows with confusion. "How do you know my name?"

He smirks at me and turns his back on me once again. I don't fucking like it. I don't like being ignored.

I reach out to grasp his arm. I shouldn't. I know I shouldn't, but something is telling me he'll allow it. Probably the same something that has my core soaked with arousal.

He turns sharply and grabs my wrist. "That's not a good idea." He doesn't let go as the words drip from his mouth with a threat. He walks toward me and I find myself taking a step back. My back hits the brick wall of a building and it makes my heart thud in my chest.

"I just wanna talk." I say the words through the hint of fear I'm feeling. His eyes hold a look of hunger, but also a dark look that has me questioning my instincts. Maybe I was wrong about him.

"Well, I don't." He releases my wrist and walks away again. My heart sinks in my chest, and I hate myself for feeling like I've failed. I can't rely on Thomas alone. I know that, but somehow there's more to this ache in my chest than just losing a lead. His rejection hurts.

I watch his back as he walks away, and the hurt turns to anger. He's not going to blow me off like that. I'm not giving up that easily. I walk faster to catch up to him. I'm shorter than him, and he's walking fast, but I quicken my steps until I'm right behind him. I *need* to know. I just need him to answer one question.

I grab his arm just enough to get his attention and pull away before he can touch me again. He opens his mouth to tell me off again, but I blurt out the question I've been dying to ask him since I first saw him at the station. "Abram Petrov, is he dead?"

The anger on his face morphs into curiosity as he tilts his head, looking me up and down.

"It's a simple question." I swallow thickly as a lump grows in my throat. I already know when he says yes, I'm going to want more answers. I'm going to want proof. I clench my fists and make sure I keep my voice down as I say, "I need to know if he's dead."

"Is that what this is for you? Revenge on Petrov? Is that why you're so damn stubborn?" he asks, like I'm being a petulant child and he finds it comical.

"He's why my sister's dead, asshole. You can at least tell me if he's dead."

Remorse flashes in his eyes as he answers, "I wish I could, but I even if I knew one way or the other, I can't say shit to you. You're a cop, remember?"

"You can tell me." My eyes plead with him. For the first time since I graduated, I wish I wasn't a cop. It never occurred to me that being a cop would close doors I'd need to go through to get to him. At the time, it was the most obvious way to move forward. I never thought twice about it until I got here.

He presses his lips into a straight line and looks at me for a moment, considering. I don't budge. I won't. I need to know.

"You think I'm stupid?" he asks, and I can see that he's gearing up for a showdown, but that's not what I want.

"You're not stupid, I don't think that at all. I'm not wired or anything. You can just nod. I swear." My words fly out in desperation.

"I'd have to strip you down to make sure you weren't. Is that what you want, little miss good girl?" A wave of arousal soaks my pussy as he leans into me. My mind starts fantasizing about things it shouldn't.

"I'm not a good girl. And if that's what it would take." I say the words before I can regret them. It's so fucking wrong. Would I really do that? Would I lower myself to stripping for him? I don't know if I'd go through with it. His eyes heat with lust, and I start to think it's a real possibility.

"No, you're not a good little girl at all, are you?" His smile widens as he takes a step back. "You're such a *bad* girl." He's mocking me. Fucking prick. I bite my tongue and watch as he turns away. My ego takes a huge fucking hit.

I turn my back on him and take a left into an alley between a convenience store and a barber shop. I know my car is parked somewhere on the next street over, parallel to this one. I don't pay attention to the men at the corner when I turn, but I sure as fuck hear them walking behind me.

Fuck!

I shouldn't have gotten so damn emotional. What the hell was I thinking? I listen to the crunch of the gravel beneath their shoes as I pass a large dumpster. I'm certain there are three. Maybe four. I'm halfway through the alley when I hear their steps pick up.

My hand drops to my gun. I'm ready for this shit. I didn't graduate at the top of my class for nothing. This is the first time I've been faced with a real-life situation like this, though. The realization makes my confidence slip as I take three large strides and turn on my heels. My gun flies out in front of me as I face three men. Two are in black hoodies, and the other one is wearing a bright green t-shirt and black jeans. I take it all in. Their heights, their weights, every bit of information I can. It's second nature at this point from all of my training.

I can feel my face heating and my body needing to tremble with fear, but I ignore it. Adrenaline flows through my blood, and the only thing I can hear is the sound of my heart beating chaotically in my chest. I swear I can feel it trying to climb up my throat.

They smile at me, like they think it's cute that I've got a gun. Like they expected me to turn around with it aimed at them. It sends a bolt of fear through me. I don't like that they knew this was coming. It means they don't care and they decided it was worth the risk. Shit, maybe that's why they followed me down here. Maybe it's obvious I'm a cop because of the way I talked to Thomas. I bet they were watching. Fuck, fuck, fuck!

I rock hesitantly on my heels, not liking the situation. I'm outnumbered, and they're looking for a fight.

One takes a step toward me and moves his hand toward his waistband. My heart slams to a stop and a cold sweat takes over every inch of my body.

"Hands up!" He continues to approach me, and I yell out again to make sure he hears me clearly. At the same time, I lift up my shirt with my left hand so he can see my badge. "Hands up!" I'm surprised I'm so composed, but I have been trained for this. I've prepared myself for this situation. "I am a police officer and I *will* fire. Put your hands where I can see them."

My left hand steadies on the butt of the gun and I watch as they show no signs of letting up. They don't give a fuck that I'm a cop, or that I've got a gun. As I prepare to shoot this prick in his hand as he reaches for his gun, I see a movement in the back of the alley.

I can't get distracted, not now. I focus, and I shoot that fucker as he grips his gun.

Chapter 7

Tommy

I almost flinch as her gun goes off. I've been around God knows how many guns going off, so I never flinch. It never bothers me. But I didn't see it coming. I guess it's just something about a cute little thing like her, I don't know what, but I underestimated her. The lowlife clutches at his hand, blood flowing freely from the wound, and he actually drops to the ground. Like a little bitch. She turns to face the other thug, but he's quick enough to close the distance between them and grab her arm.

I don't fucking like it. My blood heats, and I stride quickly to get there before shit gets out of hand. Adrenaline pumps through my veins as I grab the third guy by the nape of his neck and slam his head into the wall. I hear a loud thud and a partial scream as I take a swing and hit him square on the nose. I know it's broken. His eyes roll back in his head, and his body goes limp. I wait a second, watching to make sure his chest rises and that he's still breathing.

It does. The fucker's just knocked out, not dead. Blood leaks out of his nostrils and pools above his lip before dripping down his face and onto the pavement. He's gonna have a busted up nose and two black eyes, but he'll fucking live.

My heart beats loud in my ears as her gun goes off, hitting nothing but the brick wall and then falling to the ground with a loud bang. My surroundings go quiet and everything seems to happen in slow-motion as I take in the scene.

She's struggling with the second asshole. The first is crawling toward his gun that dropped a few feet in front of him. What a fucking pussy. The bullet passed right through his hand. I yank him backward and lift him up so I can stare that fucker in the eyes. They widen with recognition, and then fear.

He should know who I am. Everyone here knows who we are. And they know not to piss us off, either.

"Get the fuck out of here." I toss him backward like he's nothing and watch as he scrambles off. He's still clutching his hand like it's gonna fall off if he lets go. He tries to go to his friend, but that's not going to fly. I want them all separated. I want them to feel alone and scared, so they think twice about ganging up on someone else on my turf.

"Leave him." He looks back at me for a split second before taking off. Fucking prick.

I turn back to watch as Tonya knees her perp in the gut and then smashes an elbow into his jaw, blood flying from his mouth. Damn. It looks like it fucking hurt.

I walk slowly toward them, not sure if I want to interfere or not. I admire her strength. And honestly, I'm getting pretty fucking turned on watching her beat the shit out of him. The guy scoots on his butt away from her and she crawls to her gun, picking it up and pointing it at him. She's leaning back slightly and her legs are parted. She looks hot as fuck with her hair a little messed up, and her cheeks flushed.

I can tell she's out of breath because of the the heaving movements of her chest. But she's calm on the surface. I stand back and wait to see what she's going to do. She's got this shit. She kicked his ass.

"Don't move, or I'll shoot." The fucker looks up at her with daggers in his eyes and a bloody nose; he's clearly pissed that she got the best of him. She reaches into her pocket for her phone, and I have to put an end to it. I can't let her call for backup. I look at her and shake my head no.

"Give me your wallet." I walk closer and motion for her to put her phone away. She looks hesitantly at me, but she listens and slips it back into her pocket.

I have to admit that earns her a little brownie point from

me. I like her obeying me. She's a cop, she has power, she can obviously kick some ass. But she obeyed me. I fucking love that. My dick loves it too and I have to work hard not to palm my growing erection.

I watch as she slowly gets up off the ground and brushes the dirt off her ass. She doesn't look shaken up at all. She looks pissed.

The dumbfuck looks at me like he's not sure who I'm talking to. I reach down and grab him by the shirt. I pull him up and speak through clenched teeth. "Don't make me ask again."

I toss him backward and he lands hard on his ass. He doesn't waste a second as he pulls out his wallet, holding it up for me to take.

"I don't have any cash. I got nothing on me." I open up his wallet and take out my phone to take a picture of his driver's license.

"This your current address?" I ask. Fear flashes in his eyes, and the blood drains from his face.

"Answer me!" I yell louder than I should, but it doesn't make Tonya flinch.

"Y--yes," he stutters out.

"What were you planning to get out of this," I look the fucker's license and chuckle, "Earl?" I crouch down so I can look this fucker in his eyes. "What were you hoping to get from messing with her?"

"Nothin'!" He's quick to deny everything and I just tilt my

head and get ready to beat this fucker to a bloody pulp. I don't have a problem getting people to talk.

I smash my fist against his jaw so fucking quick he didn't see it coming. I hear Tonya take a step back and I look at her from the corner of my eyes. She looks back at me with no fear. She's watching me. I need to keep that in mind. I straighten my back as the little prick wipes the blood from his mouth and tries to figure out whether or not he should be looking at me. The coward doesn't even try to look me in the eyes. I have to tame the animal in me that wants to rip him to shreds. I should, he earned it, but I can't, knowing a cop is watching my every move. Even if it is for her. I'm not sure I trust this broad. My jaw ticks. I *shouldn't* fucking trust this broad. Ever.

"I like this broad, and I don't like that you fucked with her. You understand what I'm saying?"

"It w--won't happen again." He stutters again, and I swear to God I smell piss.

"Damn right it won't." I toss his wallet back to him. "Get the fuck out of here."

As he walks away, nearly stumbling over his own two feet, Tonya walks closer to me and says, "I could've handled it myself."

I look at her with a bit of disbelief. My eyes roam her body. She's a bit scuffed up. She takes the hair tie out of her hair and pulls it back up, casually tying it into a ponytail. Like messing up her hair is the worst thing that happened.

When she looks back at me, I see her true emotions in her

eyes. She's pushing down the fear and anxiety I know she's feeling. I know it well, because I do that shit, too. I walk over and stand close to her, wanting to hold her, but knowing I shouldn't.

I shouldn't have even come down here. I'd ended it. But I saw those pricks and the way they looked at her. I wasn't letting that shit happen.

I don't care what Vince has to say about it.

"You could have, but you didn't have to." Her eyes flash with surprise and then sadness. I try to lighten the mood by saying, "I couldn't let you have all the fun."

I put my hand on the small of her back and lead her out of the alley, onto the sidewalk. There's no one out this late. I doubt anyone around here called the cops either. I take out my phone and text Nicky about the prick we left behind. He'll clean it up. The fuckers will live, but they'll know never to do stupid shit like that in our territory again.

As soon as I hit send, she seems to come to her senses and tries to turn back.

"I have to call for backup," she says as she turns to look back down the alley. Fuck that. She's not calling anyone. I spin her around in my arms and look her right in her eyes.

"It didn't happen. Nothing happened." A moment passes between us, like she's weighing her options. Finally, she nods her head slightly with understanding, but I know she doesn't like it.

She looks past me at the passed out fucker in the alley.

"Don't worry about him," I tell her as I grab her by the arm. "He'll live."

She doesn't put up much of a fight. She just looks at me with curiosity on her face. It's not good that she's curious, but at least she's smart enough not to ask questions. I'm surprised how she lets me lead her out onto the street. She doesn't care that I'm practically manhandling her.

That's another thing I like. She obeys me, and she likes my hands on her. Fuck, I can't help how much that turns me on. My dick is begging to get inside her. Damn it. I really was going to listen. I have to fucking listen. I try to will away my erection, but it's not doing anything but getting harder for her.

As we get to the end of the sidewalk, her eyes steady on a parking lot across the street. I recognize her car and let her lead a bit so she doesn't realize I know that's where we're going.

I push my luck a little further and wrap my arm around her waist. She doesn't lean in, but she doesn't pull away. I'm fine with that. I like feeling her body up against me. I know being out with her like this is a risk. If Vince sees it, he's not going to believe I'm not trying to get into her pants.

Shit, I can't even believe I'm not trying to get into her pants. I have enough willpower to say no though. I'm just taking a little more than I should. After seeing her take care of that asshole, though, fuck it was sexy as fuck. How could I not put my hands on her? I wanna teach her a lesson though. She shouldn't have gone down that alley.

If she was mine, I'd have her ass red by now.

I always thought I wanted a good girl, but this woman is a bad, bad girl in need. I look down at her and watch as her eyes dart around the parking lot as we near her car. It's the same shit she always does at night. I don't like it.

"You alright?" I ask.

"Fine," she says simply, and pulls away as she takes her keys from her back pocket. I let her go as she unlocks her car and turns her body toward me. I have to remind myself she's a cop, and that's not okay.

She looks up at me and I can't help but feel like a dick for holding that against her. Besides, it's fucking hot. I wanna test her, I wanna push and see what I can get away with. After all, she left that prick in the alley for my men to clean up. I wonder how far she'd let me go before she did anything.

I put my hand on her hip and push her ass against the car.

Her eyes widen as she gasps, and I swear her thighs clench. She bites down on her bottom lip, looking up at me with a hint of fear, but mostly lust. Fuck me, but I fucking want her. I lean down and take in her sweet smell, then dip my head into the crook of her neck. I want her so fucking bad, but I can't.

I pull back and look down at her again. I get a glimpse of her badge, and suddenly she's not the hot bad girl who needs a lesson. She's the woman who sat in the interrogation room. This is a woman who may be setting me up, but all I can see is a woman who needs my touch.

Her eyes close and she tilts her head just a bit. Enough that it makes me want to cup her chin in my hand and start out nice and slow. That's how I'd do it. I'd be sweet and gentle, let her lips mold to mine. I'd make sure she was relaxed after that shit that happened. I'd make sure it was completely out of her mind. And then I'd take her wrists in my hand, pin them to the car and push this raging erection that won't let up into her thigh so she'd know how much I want her. I can see it all playing out before my eyes.

But I can't have it.

I have direct orders to stay away. And usually that doesn't mean shit, but Vince is right. This broad could be playing me. I don't think she is, but she could be. All this tension I feel between us could be her doing, just so she can find something to pin against me.

My dick jumps in my jeans thinking about pinning her against her car and slipping those jeans down so I can feel if she wants me as much as I want her. My eyes roam her body in appreciation and when I look back up, her eyes are open.

She looks vulnerable and I take the chance to give her a little smirk and a pat on the ass. She may be using me and until I'm sure she's not, I'm not giving her anything. Even if my body is fucking begging me to indulge.

She pouts and then narrows her eyes. But I saw that little pout. Sexiest fucking look a woman's ever given me. Then she swings her door open and nearly punches me right in the dick. She smirks back with a tilt of her head before climbing in.

I grab the door before she can shut it and that smirk on her gorgeous face fucking vanishes. I wanna say something smart, something that an asshole would say to push her away, but there's a look in her eyes that's telling me it'd really fucking hurt her. And that's something I don't want to do. I should push her away. I know I should. But she just had three fuckers come after her and she's not showing any signs of giving a fuck when I know she is.

It's hard for me to understand. I'm not used to women taking shit like that. Not in our family. They stay out of *familia* business. It's an unspoken rule. Women are off-limits. Yet she chose a career that puts her in harm's way every fucking day.

My grip tightens on the edge of the door. I have no right not to like it. It's her decision and she's not mine, but I'll be damned if I say I'm okay with what happened.

I ask her again, making sure the concern comes through, "You sure you're okay?"

She blinks a few times as if gauging whether I really do give a shit before she answers. She nods her head and replies, "Yeah, I'm fine."

She puts her hand on the door to close it, but before she does, she looks up and asks, "Is he dead?"

She keeps asking the same question and I don't like it.

Cops ask questions. And answering that particular one could mean trouble for me. The concern is wiped off my face like it was never fucking there.

"You have a nice night, Officer Kelly," I say as I turn my back on her and walk away. I get a few feet from her when I hear the car door shut and her engine roar to life.

As she drives away, the anger and disappointment settle in. What the fuck was I thinking? She could've handled herself; I could've stayed back and made sure she was fine after the fact. Instead I got shit on my hands that she could arrest me for.

But she didn't. I'm not sure I trust it though. I sure as fuck don't trust her. As I walk away with more resolve to keep my distance and listen to the orders Vince gave me, my phone goes off. It's a text from Vince.

Why the fuck did you need Nicky?

Fuck.
This is exactly why I need to stay the fuck away from her.

Chapter 8

Tonya

I still don't understand what happened. I park my car under the light and look up at my steps. I sit there for a moment. It's a moment too long. I should get inside. I'm quick like I always am, and I walk straight upstairs. It's not till the keys fall into the glass bowl on the end table that I realize my hand is shaking.

I take a deep breath and try to calm myself. It happens a lot. I thought it would stop eventually. It's a reaction from the adrenaline and endorphins wearing off. It's not shock, but it's not okay, either. I see it as a weakness and I hate it.

I sink into the sofa and try to calm myself down. I can do this. I *have* to do this. Other women are strong enough. Fuck, if a man can do it, so can I. Men use brute strength, while women use leverage, and brains. I truly believe that. But damn, this is fucking hard. It's so goddamned hard. I thought police academy was rough. And it was. But real-life situations are scary as fuck.

Hand-to-hand combat is its own kind of beast. It's terrifying at times. Women are worse than men. Way worse. Men sometimes only go a blow or two. They wanna prove a point. I've seen them tear each other to pieces in front of me. Even the bang of my gun going off didn't pull them off each other. But that's rare.

Women are the opposite. When they go at it, they're going for damage. They want blood. Humiliation. They want to scar their opponent and ruin them. They go for the face and eyes, their hair. Anywhere visible. I've pulled men apart on my own before. Men stronger than me. But it's nothing like pulling women apart. They go for damage and they don't give a fuck who goes down with them.

I swallow thickly, trying to just calm down. It only takes a moment to think back to when things were easier. I remember why I'm doing this. Why it's worth it to continue.

I remember playing with my sister in the front yard with chalk. Her graduation from nursing school. Talking to her on the phone. I remember the last time I heard her voice. I hear the conversation echo in my head.

"You're such a dork, Melissa. You need to go have some fun," I say to her.

"I'm seriously fine at home, you go ahead without me."

"You are truly missing out. Like you have no idea." I can't believe she'd hold herself back again; she's gotta learn to live a little. "There's nothing wrong with going clubbing. You gotta get some from time to time."

"Oh my God, don't talk like that!" she admonishes me with a hushed tone.

"Why?" I ask.

"'Cause you sound like a slut!" I can hear the humor in her voice.

"So?" We both laugh at my joke. "You just need to loosen up is all I'm saying."

"Well I'm not like you, Tonya." I can hear a little disappointment in her voice and I hate it. "I don't have that confidence." I want to tell her she should. I want to tell her she's beautiful and deserving of happiness and that includes meeting up with me to go out for drinks. But I don't want to upset her. I don't want to be pushy. So I don't say anything at all.

And because of that, I missed out on one more night that I could've had with her.

She really was a prude and an 'inside person' as she used to say. She didn't read the same smutty books as me or enjoy the dirty jokes I liked. But she didn't hold it against me, either. She never judged me. I'm guilty of judging her, though. I assumed she'd meet a doctor and make lots of babies and drive a minivan in just a few years. I teased her all the time about it.

To her, it was a dream. To me, it's a fucking nightmare.

I shake my hands out and wipe away the stray tears as I walk to the fridge. I grab the opened bottle of wine from the bottom shelf, a cabernet. I take a glass from the cabinet above the sink and ignore the dishes. They can wait. I just need to settle in a bit first.

I close my eyes and watch the scene from the alley play out again. I did everything right, flashed my badge, said hands up. First guy reaches, I shoot him in the hand. Second guy comes at me, but I'm too slow. I play the scene over while I fill the glass about halfway. Both hands were on the gun. There was nothing I could do with the other one coming after me. I needed a hand free.

I replay it over and over, trying to come up with a better strategy. But I don't think there was one. I definitely did right by going for the armed one first. Maybe if I'd used the butt of the gun to smash in the second fucker's nose, that may have been more effective. I rewind a bit in my mind. I should've turned sooner, before I'd gone so far down the alley. Fuck me, I just shouldn't have gone down there in the first place. That was fucking stupid.

Thomas is why my head is all fucked up. He does something to me. He makes me stupid, that's his fucking superpower. He blinds me from all this shit that I've trained myself to do. He makes me feel...safe, in a weird way. I feel unstoppable around him. That's not a good thing. Maybe it's because he gives me hope. When I think about the end to all this shit, when I think about having some sort of closure, I see him there. I can see him handing it to me. Telling me Petrov's dead. That I don't have to face my demons, because he's already killed them for me. Maybe it's my way of dealing with the failure of not finding Petrov. Maybe I've made it all up.

I don't know, I'm not a fucking shrink.

I tip the glass back and drain it. Mmm, I love the taste. I set the glass down on the counter and strip as I make my way to my bedroom. Most of my things are still in boxes. I need to make time to put that shit away. I toss the clothes into the hamper. At least that's not overflowing. Score one for me.

My feet patter against the tiled floor as I turn the water on to fucking-scorching, just how I like it. I look at my face in the mirror as the water heats and steam starts to fill the stall.

I look back at a stranger.

This isn't who I used to be.

I look... tired. That's exactly how I look. And I am, I'm so damn tired. I'm lonely and angry. And fucking sad and miserable.

The need for justice. The need for vengeance. They've taken over a part of me that I miss. But they are needs. I need to know if Petrov is dead. If he's not, I won't stop. I hate that I've come to the end of this lead, all because Thomas won't give me an inch.

Suddenly, I wish I had more on his ass. I want something to make him talk. I need him to tell me. I could use what happened today. But that'd be so fucking wrong. I feel like a bitch for even thinking it. Maybe this anger that's driving me, this desire to fuck him over until I get what I need, maybe that's what fuels Harrison every fucking day.

The realization snaps me out of my thoughts. No, I can't do that. I shouldn't want that.

But I know that Thomas knows. He could tell me where Petrov is, or if he's dead. I know he can.

I step into the shower deciding I need to push him just a bit more. After all, I've given him something. I could have called it in, the scene today. I *should* have called it in.

But he didn't have to do it. He didn't have to help me.

Oh fuck, I'm such a bitch. I never even thanked him.

I let the hot water hit my skin and fucking hate the obsession that's taken me over. Who am I? I shake my head and try to shake off all these unwanted feelings, all these horrible thoughts. I don't like the person I've become. I just want it all to stop.

If only he'd help me.

Chapter 9

Tommy

I look out of the peephole and curse under my breath. This broad has a fucking death wish. I stand in front of the closed door and listen as the loud knock echoes in my apartment. Fucking hell. She just won't let it be.

This is what I get for wanting to find out more about this broad. Vince already bitched at me for involving myself. He couldn't hold it against me though. Not when I fed him a little lie about how she was shaken up from how they'd roughed her up.

I really think she was a bit messed up from it. But I may have exaggerated some to get myself off the hook.

I decided I was done with this that night, done with her.

I should threaten a restraining order. I could do it, too. I've told her I don't want to talk.

And now she's standing outside my door.

"I know you're home, Thomas," she yells from the other side. "I just wanna talk." I roll my eyes. No shit. That's all this broad wants from me. *'Cause she's a cop.*

I need to send her away. I need to do it now.

I swing the door open and it stops her fist in the air. I look at her clenched hand pointedly until she lowers it and then I stare at her. I keep my face impassive. None of that bullshit I gave into before. This needs to end.

"You wanna talk, go ahead and talk," I tell her in a no-nonsense tone.

She opens her mouth and then closes it. She clears her throat and looks to the ground before looking back up at me. "Thank you. I just wanted to say thank you."

I stare at her, not quite understanding. I'm surprised by her sweetness. It catches me off guard. Which isn't a good thing.

"For helping me with those guys." She closes her eyes and takes a deep breath. "I never thanked you for stepping in. It would've really sucked if you hadn't." *It would have sucked.* That's putting it mildly.

I should just stare. I shouldn't respond. She'd get the message loud and clear, but I can't do that. I look past her and give a curt nod as I say, "No problem."

She noticeably swallows and asks, "May I come in?"

"No." It's easy shutting that down. The only reason I'd bring her in here is to fuck her. And that's not going to happen. My dick doesn't like that answer and starts hardening in my pants. I clench my jaw, trying to get it to go down. I'm only in a pair of sweats. She's gonna see how fucking hard I am for her. Fuck it, I still can't have her. Doesn't fucking matter if she knows I want her or not.

I need to push her away.

"You're in the wrong part of town, Tonya," I say, keeping my eyes on her with my voice low.

A smile spreads slowly across her face, making her look gorgeous as fuck. She cocks a brow and tries to suppress the laugh that I can practically hear escaping from those full lips of hers. "You're kidding, right?" She's not really asking though, and she has a point. I'm a scary fucker, but it's not like I live in the rough part of town.

"You know what I mean." She should know not to fuck with me. Maybe I've been too easy on her. I've given her this idea that I won't hurt her, and I'm her pal. But I'm not her buddy. She should be fucking careful around me. She should be scared of me.

She rolls her eyes at my words and it's the last straw.

"You think you're such a bad ass bitch, don't you?" I walk into her space, pushing her farther out into the hallway.

She seems taken aback by my tone, and it takes a moment for her to square her shoulders. I can see her changing before my eyes. Like she just realized who I am, and that she's a cop. She may think she doesn't have to take any shit from me, but I'm about to prove her wrong.

"You think you can play this good girl act with me, but I know who you really are."

She looks confused and then pissed. "I never said I was a good girl, and I'm not putting on an act." She speaks through clenched teeth with her hands balled at her side. It really pisses her off when I call her that. That's good to know. I like pissing her off and getting her riled up.

"So what? You're a bad girl then? Just like I said, you think you're a bad ass. You're not."

She huffs a laugh and rolls her eyes. She literally doesn't give a shit. I need to instill fear into this broad. I've given her too much length on her leash.

I look her in her eyes and lower my voice. "I could fuck you raw in the front of this building, and no one would stop me. No one would say shit to me."

Her lips part, and her eyes soften with lust at my words. Fuck me, that's so fucking hot. That's not at all the reaction I expected. I anticipated disgust. I would think she'd pull out the cop card. But she doesn't.

"You'd like that, wouldn't you?" I ask as I grip her hips and turn her around to pin her to the wall next to my open door. "'Cause you're such a bad girl." I lower my lips to her neck and whisper in her ear. My lips barely touch her. "You'd love it so fucking much, you'd cum on my dick as I fucked your greedy cunt however I wanted."

I shove her back against the wall. I'm not gentle, but only because I can see how much she likes it rough. I grab her ass with both hands and hold her against the wall with my hips. My hard dick pushes against her thigh, digging into her. I can see the moment she realizes she's about to get fucked. Her eyes widen and she pushes her hands against my chest. I pull back slightly, but my hands and hips keep her in place.

My heart beats wildly in my chest. My blood's laced with desire and races with a primal need to fuck her against the wall. She'd fucking love it. We both want it.

I lean forward and barely hear her say, "Ssst." She knows she should say it, but she hasn't yet. She likes me pushing her boundaries.

"Stop?" I ask with a lopsided grin. "Is that what you were gonna say?" She presses her lips together and turns her head to the side, refusing to look at me and refusing to answer. I heard it on the tip of her tongue. But she doesn't want this to stop. She wants to be impaled on my dick.

"You'd better fucking say it, Tonya." Her eyes whip up to mine with a flash of anger. She doesn't like me telling her what to do. Good. It's going to be fun getting her so worked up. I love it already.

I wrap my hand around her throat and give her a gentle squeeze. My left hand grabs hold of her thigh and she spreads her legs for me. I cup her pussy and rock my palm against her clit. I can feel how hot and wet she is. Her eyes go half-lidded, and her lips part with a small moan of pleasure. It's the sexiest fucking thing I've ever heard. I bend my head down and hesitate just a second before taking her bottom lip in between my teeth.

This is dangerous. At first it felt like a game. But the more I push, the more she gives me. I'm already addicted, and I haven't even had a taste of her yet. I should stop this before it begins, but I can't. I want her, and now that I know how much she wants me, I'm taking her.

I'm going to have to fuck this broad out of my system. Just once. Just once, so I can satisfy this beast clawing at me to fuck her into submission.

I lower my lips to the crook of her neck and bite down hard enough so she knows I won't be gentle. She rocks her hips and rubs her hot pussy against my dick. Fuck, yes. I growl into her ear, "Get your ass inside."

I pull back and stare into her green eyes. They spark with a challenge. "Thought you said you could fuck me out here." My dick jumps in my pants.

"Bad girl." I back away so I'm not touching her. "Get inside." I see the defiance in her eyes. She fucking loves this. She's coming alive with my touch, and I love that I can do this to her. She bites down on her lip and looks to the stairs. For a moment, one split second, I think she's going to leave, but then her cute ass starts walking inside, and I know I've got her.

After I close and lock her door, I grip her waist and lead her to the bedroom. I'm not wasting any time. I don't want to give either of us a second to think and realize what a fucking disaster this is.

I kick the door shut behind me and give her another command. "Strip." I fucking love how she turns on her heels and looks back at me like she's debating on giving me a hard time.

"You have this coming. For teasing me like that. You better take them off before I rip them off of you." Her mouth parts and the moan I was fantasizing about hearing finally hits my ears. "I don't give a fuck if you have to walk back home naked." Yes. Yes I really fucking do give a shit, but that gets her ass moving to obey.

Her hands slowly remove her jeans, and then her top. She reaches around behind her to remove her bra, but I can't wait any longer.

I pick her ass up, a cheek in each hand and let my knees hit the edge of the mattress. She's quick to wrap her legs around mine. Her heels dig into my ass as my lips crush hers. I fall onto my bed with her beneath me and push down my sweats. My cock smacks against her clit as it bounces out, and the force of it makes her break our kiss. She moans into the hot air and it fuels me to grip my dick in my hand and smack it against her swollen nub. I want to hear that sound again and again. Her back arches and her head digs into the mattress. I move my cock through her folds from her entrance to her clit, making sure to watch her body for her reaction. She fucking loves this. She's loving what I'm doing to her.

She still isn't looking at me though, and I don't like that. I want her eyes on me as I sink deep into her heat. I line my cock up and then grip her chin in my hand. She looks back at me with half-lidded eyes. She's already so close. My bad girl is dying to be fucked.

I hold her gaze as I slowly push into her tight cunt. Fuck, she feels so fucking good. My thick cock stretches her walls as I slowly thrust deep inside her. Her eyes widen and her lips form a perfect "o". I'd smirk at her if I could, but I can't. I'm lost in how fucking good she feels.

I rock into her once, twice, and then a third time, keeping my pace slow and steady with short, shallow strokes letting her adjust to my size and then I thrust into her hard enough that the bed slams against the wall. She screams out and I capture her screams of pleasure with my kiss. My fingertips dig into her hips, holding her in place as I continue mercilessly fucking her into the mattress. The bed groans and creaks as I pound into her pussy with a relentless pace.

Her thighs tighten around my hips as she bites down on her lip to keep from screaming out from the intense pleasure.

The bed smacks against the wall with each thrust. As I fuck her harder it gets louder, and I fucking hate that she looks up at the headboard. It was only a glance, but it's enough that

I want to drag her ass onto the floor and fuck her there. She can hear the creaking and groaning and it's distracting her. It pisses me off. That's not going to fucking happen. I want her so far gone that she can't think about anything but my dick giving her the release she so desperately needs.

I pick her ass up in one hand and press my thumb against her clit. I push down hard and ignore her body trying to thrash in my arms. I don't stop. I don't let up on my ruthless thrusts as I circle her clit, taking her higher and higher. Her head thrashes from side to side as her pussy spasms around my dick. I feel her hot arousal and groan as the sound of my dick slamming into her gets louder and messier. I fucking love that I made her cum. I want it again. I want more of her.

I ride through her orgasm and push her to another level of ecstasy. I rub her clit with the rough pad of my thumb and keep up my pace. My spine tingles and my toes curl, wanting my release, but I hold it back, waiting for her to go off again. I need it again. I want to take her over the edge. She claws at the comforter and screams out as I pinch her clit.

Only when I feel her body trembling and see her back bow with her own orgasm, only then do I let the sensation wash over me. I cum violently deep inside her and groan into the crook of her next as the pleasure runs through every inch of my body. I brace my forearms above her head, and we sink into the mattress as I pump short, shallow thrusts until I'm completely spent and have nothing left.

I roll onto my back and pull her close to me while we both catch our breath. It's been a long time, a really long fucking time, but it's never felt like *that* before. More than anything, I feel triumphant. Like I've tamed the untamable.

I let a few minutes go by for my heart to calm down. You'd think I held my breath the whole fucking time. My lips travel along her shoulder and I leave a sweet kiss on the tender part of her neck, just behind her ear before getting up. She was so fucking good, better than I fucking hoped she'd be.

I need to get her something to clean up with.

When I get back from the bathroom, she's sitting up on the bed holding the comforter across her chest. Her hair's a mess, her lips are swollen from my kiss, and her skin looks radiant. She looks like she got fucked, and it looks damn good on her.

I pass her the washcloth and pretend like I'm looking away while I pull on my boxers.

She rolls off the bed and sashays her ass in my face. I know she did that shit on purpose. I smack my hand playfully across that perky, lush ass, and smile as she jumps and turns around to face me. A deep red blush colors her cheeks as she smiles shyly back at me.

That's when it hits me.

This broad is getting to me. I watch as she grabs her clothes. All the bits of happiness leave me in an instant. I didn't check for a wire. Fuck. Fuck, how could I forget she's a cop?

I didn't say anything, though. I know I didn't. I replay the scene in my head.

It's like snapping back to reality. I don't know what the fuck happened.

Shit. Maybe she wanted this. She wanted to get close to me. Fuck. Fuck. I keep fucking this up. I'm so drawn to her. I run a hand down my face in exasperation. What the hell was I thinking? I keep losing my shit when she's around.

I look at her from across the room as she pulls her jeans up and over her sweet ass. Fuck, even right now as I'm telling myself this is wrong, my dick is hardening at the chance to be inside her again.

"This shit can't happen." I say the words before I forget that I need this to be over. "It can't happen again."

She turns to face me with a look of shock and hurt. But she's quick to cover it up. It fucking kills me. A weight pushes against my chest. It fucking hurts. I hate that I hurt her. "You're right. Sorry it happened." She talks clearly, and with a hint of sarcasm, but doesn't face me. She sounds fucking pissed, but there's an undertone of sadness. She's doing what she does best, and masking her true feelings.

I walk over to her to hold her, or apologize, or something--I don't know what, but she makes a beeline for her purse and then starts heading to the door. It fucking hurts, but that's what I get. What did I expect, opening my mouth and ruining it?

We were playing house though. Caught up in something

that doesn't exist.

"I'm not kicking you out." I talk to her back as she walks out on me. I may as well have kicked her out though. I close my eyes and take a deep breath. This needs to go down like this. She needs to be pissed at me. But I don't want that.

This is all so fucked.

She turns to face me as I walk up behind her before she can open the door. I want to say something to her. I don't know what. I just don't want her to leave like this.

"Don't worry, it won't happen again." Her voice is hard and full of menace, but her eyes are glassy with tears. It fucking guts me.

"Stop it, Tonya. It's not like that." She turns her back to me to open the door, but I put my hand above hers to keep it from opening. She turns around and I cage her in. She closes her eyes to avoid my stare.

"Stop it. You know I didn't mean it like that." I talk with a gentle tone and try to calm her down. But her defenses are way up. She's not giving me anything. "You don't want this anyway. You're a cop. I'm suspect in your case for fuck's sake."

"You didn't do it," she says calmly. Her admission shocks me. If she knows I didn't do it, what the fuck is she after me for? "You're right though. This shouldn't have happened." She opens her eyes and speaks calmly, "I want to leave now."

There's no emotion left. No sadness, no disappointment, no anger. She's got her mask on, and she's not giving me anything.

I should make her open up. I shouldn't let her leave like this.

But it's what's best for both of us. She's a cop, and I'm mobbed up. This shit should've never happened.

"Alright." I stand back and let her open the door. I fucking hate that I feel anything for her. She's a cop. I have to keep repeating it in my head. I have to remember I can't have her. I've been ordered to stay away from her. I shouldn't have let it get this far. This is bad. I don't know what I was thinking.

"Can you just tell me one thing?" she asks, as she steps out into the hallway. "Is Petrov dead?" She looks up at me with nothing in her eyes, no emotion. Not a damn thing.

I bite the inside of my cheek fucking hating that she's asking that.

"You know I can't tell you anything. Stop asking me. I'm not gonna answer." I can't. I'd be a stupid prick to admit anything.

"Yeah, I figured. Couldn't hurt to ask one more time though." She walks down the hallway without looking back.

I feel fucking used. But what's worse is that I want to stop her. I want to tell her how he suffered. How a woman who he tortured killed him. But I can't.

Instead I stand in my doorway and listen to her steps. I grip the door jamb tighter as I hear the door open and listen as she leaves.

Fuck, I want to tell her. And that's not good. None of this is good.

Chapter 10

Tonya

I'm not gonna cry. I don't fucking cry. Sure as shit not over men. I've had a few boyfriends here and there, but that's never happened to me. It's never been a hit it and quit it situation. And sure as fuck not five minutes after cumming inside of me. Asshole. He didn't kick me out, but he could've picked a better time to start talking like that.

It was a mistake. I know that. It never should've happened. I have more restraint than that. I don't know what it is about him that makes me so weak. I cave to him, when I haven't ever caved before. I don't like it. I also don't like that he brought it up first. I was thinking it, but I was pushing it down.

It just felt so nice to be held. It's been a long time. I

feel so fucking deprived of human interaction. It's been too fucking long. I take a deep breath as I lie down on my bed. It's cold. But it feels good to just relax against the bed. I snort a humorless laugh.

I shouldn't be relaxing. I shouldn't even want that. I've lost sight of my purpose. I swore I wouldn't stop until I found Petrov and destroyed him and everyone who works for him. It's like I was wearing blinders all through the academy. I didn't even care about how much my body hurt. Nothing else mattered. I was just obsessed at taking a leap forward.

And then my huge break when the department had an opening was as if the stars had aligned. Like God was handing me my revenge on a silver platter. But then nothing. Not a fucking trace of him. The other names on my list are all dead. There are no leads. I shouldn't be relaxing, but I don't know what else to do.

It's as if I've been running as hard and as fast as I'm able, chasing a ghost. And now he's disappeared, and I'm finally taking a look around.

How did I get here? This isn't what I went to college for. This isn't what I wanted to do. My life wasn't supposed to end up like this. Even back then I wasn't really sure what I wanted, but the shit I was studying was at least interesting. All of this is just depressing as fuck.

But I owe it to my sister. She was older than me. Only by three years. She was reserved and polite. I was the handful child that always got into trouble. Maybe that's why I never got along with my mother. I don't know. But that relationship completely vanished when Melissa died. My mother couldn't take it. She's not a fighter like me.

The night Melissa didn't come back, my mom was sure she was dead. The next morning when I went looking for her, putting up signs and waiting for the police to actually do something, my mother did nothing but cry. I was pissed. She wasn't even trying. I think she buried Melissa that day. And what was left of her own soul.

Ever since I've been so fucking alone.

Melissa could've been trapped. She could have hit her head somehow and been unconscious. A million scenarios ran through my head. I knew deep inside me that she needed me. She needed *us*. Yet my mother did nothing but sob inconsolably.

I hated her then. It was like I could feel my sister's pain, and I tried so fucking hard. I looked everywhere I could. But I never would have found her. I was looking in all the wrong places.

It wasn't long after that when her body was discovered. I couldn't believe it. I couldn't imagine that someone would take her. After the shock and the sadness, all that was left was anger. I knew I had to do something.

I took a semester off school to join the groups that all promise to bring awareness to sex trafficking. I went to meetings, presentations, and counseling. But it didn't feel like enough. More than that, I saw my sister in the women who survived. I could see her in their place.

But I knew she'd never be there. She was dead. She wasn't ever going to sit in the chair across from me, and tell me what happened to her. She wasn't going to be making plans with me on how to handle simple, everyday tasks that now felt impossible. I had to stop going.

I needed to go after the man who'd led her to her death.

I feel like it was just yesterday that I'd made up my mind to chase after Petrov. Like I'd gone into a dark tunnel and sprinted through it blindly, only to emerge and not realize where it was taking me.

He may be dead. I may never get to face him. I may never even know for sure. But I won't stop.

The rest of the Valettis know something, and I can question them. Well, I can try. I know it's risky. But I have to try. I'll do anything to make sure Petrov never puts his hands on another woman. I hope he suffered. Tears leak down my face and hit the pillow beneath me. A sob tears through me, and I have no idea where it came from.

My anger is waning, knowing he may no longer be alive. What's left if I don't have the anger to hold onto? My chest feels hollow. And I can't stand the distant feeling of sadness.

I wish I knew one way or the other.

He could've at least told me. Thinking of Thomas makes the pain subside, if only for a moment. He made me weak. I enjoyed it though. I'm tired of being the strong one. I'm tired of fighting an enemy I can't even see. I'm tired of chasing ghosts.

I close my eyes and try to think of anything other than the dark past, and twisted obsession that's brought me here. I steady my breathing and see Thomas' face.

I feel his hands on my body. His lips against my neck.

"Bad girl." The memory of his deep, baritone voice sends a shiver through my body. I can imagine a time when I would have run off with him. When I would have gotten on my knees and done everything and anything he asked, just for the thrill of it.

That time's passed though. And now neither of us are in a position to allow what we did to ever happen again. My eyes pop open, realizing if he told anyone, I'd lose my job. I expect to feel fear, or shock, or anger at the thought. But I feel nothing. I don't think I'd care.

It would hurt though, for him to use it against me. He should. If I were him, I would. What we did wasn't right, and it would certainly add a level of distrust and uncertainty to the case if I got pulled off. It would severely compromise the case.

But the evidence is iffy as is. All we really have are the prints at this point. The tire tracks are circumstantial, and the witness deposition is inadmissible due to her state of mind.

The partial print is the only piece of evidence that's damning, according to the prosecutor.

There's no more evidence to collect, and everything we have

points to the Valettis ending the deal and saving the women.

I can't even fathom why Jerry is still gunning for them, unless he's hoping for the same outcome as Harrison, just in a more professional way. I guess it's professional to leverage and threat in order to get information for other cases.

The lines are blurred so much more than I ever thought they could be.

And I'm tired of looking at black and white. I rest my head into the pillow and try not to think about any of it at all. I just want to rewind time. I want to go back to the last time I saw Melissa and hold her. If I'd known then, what I know now, I'd never let her go. I don't care if it's crazy. I would do anything I could to save her.

The tears come again and I hug my pillow. I can't save her. I'll never be able to save her. My throat closes as I sniffle and try to breathe into the pillow.

She's never coming back. And nothing I'll ever do can change that.

Chapter 11

Tommy

"What the fuck is that broad thinking?" Anthony walks up behind me at the bar, and I have to turn around to face him.

He looks worried. "What are you talking about?" I ask.

"Your chick, Tonya Kelly. The cop." He says, "the cop" like I wouldn't know who he's talking about. My eyes lower to the drink in my hand. I haven't had one fucking moment go by where I didn't think about her. From the way she felt writhing beneath me, to the pissed off and hurt look when I shut it down before the situation got any worse than was necessary.

I fucking hate this. I hate that I can't get her out of my head, and I hate that I can't have her. I've never had this problem before. And I don't fucking like it.

"What's she doing?" I ask, looking past him at Vince. Vince is in the corner of the room talking to his brother over a beer. They barely come in here anymore with the kids taking up so much of their time. I hope whatever my bad girl has gotten into, it hasn't found its way back to either of them.

"She's about to get slapped with a harassment lawsuit if she keeps her shit up." I look him dead in the eyes, waiting for more. "She went to Tony's and waited for him outside his house. She keeps pushing for information." He looks over his shoulder at Vince. "She's worse than a fucking reporter."

He turns like he's gonna go tell Vince, and I stop him. My hand grips his shoulder. His forehead pinches, and his eyes narrow. "What the fuck, Tommy?"

"Don't tell him, and tell Tony to keep his mouth shut." He looks at me with disbelief. "I'll handle it," I say, standing up from my barstool.

"Are you fucking kidding me? You can't go around making threats to an officer. You aren't off the hook yet."

"That's not what I have in mind," I say under my breath.

Anthony closes his eyes and lets his head fall back. "You're fucking kidding me, Tommy. Tell me you're not fucking around with her."

"I'm not." I've never been good at lying, and I sure as shit don't like lying to him. But it's partially true.

"Good. That'd be a fucking mistake."

"Stay out of it, Anthony." I'm done with this conversation.

I turn to walk away and he doesn't stop me. I feel like a prick, but I'm going after what I want.

Before I make it to the door, Vince and Dom approach me, and I know I need to stop and hear them out. I just hope it's not about her. She really should know better; she shouldn't be doing this shit. She's gonna get herself into deep shit, and I can't fucking have that happen.

"Tommy, you alright?" Dom asks. I'm sure they can see the stress on my face. I need to man the fuck up and play it cool.

"Everything considered, I'm doing just fine." I talk easy, but the tension in my body is keeping my guard up.

"You know we got you. It's all gonna be taken care of. Soon, too. We already got the witness stuff thrown out, the prints and the tire tracks are close to being gone too, and then they won't have shit on you."

I nod my head, not really listening. I'm sure I'm gonna get off, so I'm not too worried about that. But my bad girl is gonna get herself into some deep shit, and I need to stop that. I don't want them thinking of her like they do Harrison.

"Has that bitch cop been bugging you?" Vince asks, and it takes everything in me not to make a fist and smash it into his face.

"She's not a bitch," I manage to say back, and he doesn't like that answer. Dom seems surprised and takes a step back. He doesn't get involved with this shit. I can't help that the words come out. I don't like him calling her a bitch. She may be a little rough around the edges. She's a little pushy, but she's not a bitch. Nothing about her makes me think that.

"She's still a cop though, isn't she?" Vince asks in a hushed voice.

"Yeah she is." I answer him quickly, wanting to get rid of the tense air between us.

"She still bugging you?"

I answer him honestly. "I haven't seen her in a few days."

"Haven't seen her?" he asks, tilting his head and narrowing his eyes. "What's that mean, Tommy?"

"Means she hasn't been around to bug me. She's not like the others, Vince."

"I don't like the way you're talking Tommy." Vince wraps his arms around my shoulder and leads me to the back room. "You talking like that to anyone else?"

"I haven't said shit to anyone about anything." That's always the correct answer to give.

"You sound like you've got something going on with her, Tommy. You talking to a cop?"

"Fuck no, Vince." My body goes ice cold. I can't have anyone think I'm talking to a cop. That gets your ass killed.

"If you were anyone other than my cousin, I'd be thinking twice about believing the shit coming out of your mouth right now."

"She's a woman, is all," I answer back.

"She's a cop, Tommy. You can't forget that shit. You can't

go easy on her just because she's got tits. She'll still use anything you say against you. Isn't that one of their fucking lines?"

I press my lips into a tight line and nod diligently.

"Don't fucking talk like that around anyone else. I can't have anyone thinking you've got a thing going on with the cops. They can't start spreading shit about you talking, Tommy. There's only so much I can do to squash shit like that."

He sounds desperate for me to listen to him. And I am, but only partially.

Even as he's warning me away from her, I already know I'm going to lie to him. I already know I'm not going to listen. I think I've just been waiting for a reason to go to her, and she just gave me one.

Chapter 12

Tonya

I shut the door, dropping my keys in the glass bowl on the end table, and drag my ass over to sink down on the couch. It's been a long fucking day. I wince as I scrape the wound on my arm against the rough fabric of the sofa. I suck in a deep breath through clenched teeth. Fucking asshole made me chase him through the woods, all for what? A couple hundred bucks he stole from his parents? Seriously? It fucking pisses me off. I'm so fucking tired of dealing with junkies and this stupid shit. What's worse is I know he'll be out soon. Only to get hauled back in later. I lean my head back against the couch.

I put my hands on my forehead, and try to let the stress leave me. This isn't what I thought being a cop would be like.

I shake my head and forget that shit. I knew this was going to be hard. It's not what's eating me. I know exactly why I'm all fucked up. It's because I have no leads to the only case I really care about.

My heart twists in my chest. I don't want to think about him. I've been trying to avoid it, but he keeps haunting me. I don't know what hurts worse, the fact that he could end this pain for me, or the fact that he's gotten to me. I haven't been with anyone in so long. I don't remember it feeling like this. But then again, I've never been dumped like that either.

I snort, and force my tired body off the sofa. Like we were seeing each other. As if I mattered to him.

My gut drops, and I find myself regretting it. But I can't stand that. I don't like regret. I do what feels right, and I don't do what feels wrong. It's my own insurance policy so that I never regret anything.

At any point in my past, I know whatever I was doing was exactly what I wanted. At least right then and there. And I'd be a fucking liar if I said I didn't love every minute of Tommy fucking me. I came alive under him. I smile, remembering how loud his bed was. I shake my head and open my fridge looking for a snack or something.

It sucked though, when it was over. I look at the half gallon of milk and the rest of my practically-empty fridge and frown. I close the door and try to shake off this shit feeling. I don't hold it against him. It never should've happened. But it still fucking hurt.

I'm not going to let him stop me from getting to the bottom of Petrov's case though. I'm sure as fuck going to avoid him like the plague though. I need to get him out of my head. If anyone at the station found out what happened between us, I'd be fucked.

I feel like a bitch for judging all of them and how hard they are after years of doing this shit. No wonder they look at me like I don't belong. Fuck! I lean my head against the fridge and breathe in and out slowly. I can't shake this negativity. I can't get out of my own fucking head. I'm second-guessing everything, and feeling like shit as a result. I need to stop. But I don't know how.

I slowly open my eyes as I hear a loud knock at my door.

My heart stills in my chest. I have no clue who would come over here this late at night. I wait with anxiety trickling through my limbs for a voice. But I don't hear anything. I walk silently, but quickly to the end table and pick up my gun where I left it. I hold it down and walk steadily as I hear a loud knock again.

Bang. Bang. Bang! On the third, I hear his voice say, "Open up, Tonya." Relief washes through my body and I almost put the gun down, but then I think twice.

I look at it in my hands and remember how angry the other members of the Valetti *familia* were. In two days, I've managed to piss off more men than my mom has in her entire life. That's saying something.

"I know you're in there, you may be a bad girl, but I don't want you pushing me right now." His voice doesn't come out hard, but it's not playful either. It's almost a little worried. Like he's fairly confident that I'll answer him, but scared that I won't.

I like that.

I like making him wait. Not because I don't want to answer him, I do. The wild side of me is jumping at the chance to answer him. But I also like keeping him on edge.

I put the gun down on the end table. It may be stupid, but I don't care right now. I walk to the door and unlock it. I wait a second to see if he'll open it. But he doesn't. He respects that boundary. I close my eyes and take a deep breath. I can't let myself go back to how it was before. This is going to be professional.

I open the door and curse myself as my eyes land on his hard, muscular body. Fuck, I want him. I want all of him. I close my eyes and don't open them as he speaks.

"What are you doing snooping around?" He gets right to the point, and anger rises within me. Enough so that I can stare back at him.

"Snooping around?" I'm not snooping. I'm simply trying to get answers.

"You need to knock it off." His voice is stern and admonishing. It pisses me off, but also lights something else in me. Something I need to let die.

"I don't need to do anything, and as far as you're concerned, you weren't giving me what I needed, so I had to go somewhere else." I know the double meaning there. And I hate that it slipped out. I feel fucking pathetic.

His eyebrows raise, and he looks me up and down like he's sizing me up, but I can see he's angry. "Is that so?" he says with a neutral tone.

I start backpedaling the best I can and say, "I need answers for my own sanity."

"You're a cop, you think they're going to give you anything?" He raises his voice as he continues to lay into me, "They're not like me, Tonya. They aren't going to treat you like I do."

"So they aren't going to fuck me and then toss me aside?" I'm so fucking bitter I can't help but spit it out. I don't feel any anger toward him, but apparently some part of me does.

"Is that what you want from them?" he asks.

"Fuck off, Thomas." I start to close the door. I don't have the energy for this. If he's not going to help me, fine. If he doesn't want to fuck me anymore, that's fine, too.

Thomas stops the door and pushes it open so he can lean in. "What the fuck? You trying to piss me off, Officer Kelly?" I don't like the way he's saying my name. Like he's asking if he's talking to me or someone else, someone who he doesn't trust. I've never been anything but honest with him.

"What do you want?" I ask with irritation coloring my

voice, but I'm not irritated. I'm hurt. I want him to say, "You." I want him to come in and take me. I want him to make everything better. And that realization makes me feel weak. It makes me feel sick to my stomach.

"I wanna come in and talk."

"Now you wanna talk?" I shake my head and try to push down the bit of hope growing in my chest. It's stupid. I shouldn't be hoping. This can't happen.

"You gonna let me in?" he asks, like I might actually say yes.

"No." I shake my head and open my eyes, making sure to only look at his face. The thought of him coming in here only makes me want to test whether or not he can make my bed creak and groan like he did his. This is bad. Real fucking bad.

"Why the fuck not?" He sounds all pissed off.

"'Cause I don't have to, that's why." I'm flippant as I say it.

"Don't push me, baby." He narrows his eyes at me as he says it.

"I'm not your baby. I'm not your anything." I at least have a little pride knowing that those words came out strong.

"With a mouth like that, right now you're my bad girl. That's all you are." My pussy clenches at his words. I can't help that it turns me on. But I have to remember that this can't happen. This is wrong.

"Bad things will happen if you come in here." I tell him the truth and regret it when his eyes heat with lust and his lips pull into a smirk.

"You want me that much? You really can't control yourself?" he asks with a cocky grin.

It pisses me off. And I hold on to that anger so I can push him away like I know I should.

"Fuck you!" I grab the edge of the door and try to slam it shut, but hit boot hits the door, blocking it.

For the first time ever in his presence, I feel scared. I don't know why, but a sense of danger takes ahold of every part of me, and I race to get to my gun. I grip it with both hands and point it at him as he takes a step inside.

His eyes go wide when he sees the gun pointed at him. He raises both of his hands, "Whoa, baby, what are you doing? Put the gun down."

My hands tremble slightly, and I feel so fucking insecure. I don't know what I'm doing anymore. I don't trust anything that I'm feeling. My hand starts shaking. It's never done that. I've always had control. But I've never been in this situation before, either. I don't even know why I grabbed it.

"Hey, it's alright." He keeps his hands raised. "You really want me to go? I'll go."

I don't know what I want. I slowly aim the gun down and keep my head down. I've fucked this up so fucking bad.

"I know I push you. I didn't mean to threaten you though." I watch in my periphery as he walks toward me like one would a wounded animal. And that's exactly how I feel. I'm so fucked up. So worn out and torn.

"I'd never hurt you, Tonya." I shouldn't believe him, but I do. He reaches out slowly and grabs my gun. I think about resisting, but I don't want to. He gently places it on the end table and looks at me like he doesn't know what to do with me.

He takes his gun out, making sure to point it away from me and quickly sets it on the end table next to mine.

He cups my chin in my hand. "I'm sorry I pushed you like that. I really thought you were just pushing me back."

"I don't know what I'm doing," I say weakly, and look up at him through my thick lashes.

A soft chuckle rumbles through his chest. "I don't either, baby." He lowers his lips to mine. He whispers with his full lips barely touching my own, "I won't hurt you. And I won't let anyone else hurt you, either."

I open my eyes and see sincerity in his dark stare.

"You gotta stay away, though." My gaze drops to the floor. I try to push him away, but it's a weak and useless effort.

"Not from me." His words pull me back from the defeated place I'd sunk to. "I want you. But they can't know. No one can know, and you need to stay away from them."

His chest rises and falls, and his breathing is the only thing I can hear other than my own heart thumping in my chest.

This is dangerous. It's forbidden. But I want it. I want him.

"Tell me you want me, baby." His voice is confident, but I can tell he needs the reassurance. He needs me to tell him I want him, too. And I do. I desperately want him.

"I want you." Before the last word leaves my lips, his hands grip my hips and he pulls me under him as he falls onto the sofa.

His fingers tickle my skin as they travel under my shirt, slowly lifting it up past my breasts.

"I'll make you feel better, baby."

"Yes," I whisper. Please. I need to feel better.

"You're just too tempting. I fucking need you under me." He stares at my breasts as he pulls the cup of my bra down and pinches my hardened nubs. It sends a direct shot of need to my clit.

A soft smile plays at his lips, but he looks into my eyes with concern.

"You really thought I'd hurt you?" He pulls my shirt over my head, taking the bra with it and lifts me into his lap. His arms wrap around my waist as he leans back against the sofa.

I feel ashamed, so I try to look away, but he cups my face and turns my head so I have to look at him. "Don't do that."

"I'm sorry," I say barely above a murmur. I am. I'm so damn sorry.

He smirks a bit and says playfully, "I had it coming, messing with a bad girl like you."

He takes my lips with his, and I feel every emotion crash down around me. The only one left standing is lust. I moan into his parted lips and let his hands roam my body. I need him to take me away. I need to *feel* something else.

He tosses me backward and climbs between my legs, ripping off everything in his way. I want to close my legs, but I don't. The look of hunger in his eyes keeps my legs spread wide for him. He licks his lips and gently runs a finger down my hip bone and over my clit. My body shudders under his touch, and his lips twitch into a satisfied smile as he lowers his lips to my pussy.

His deft fingers pump in and out of me while he sucks my clit. My eyes roll back in my head as my back bows and I struggle with my composure. It's so intense. Too intense. My body begs me to move away, not knowing if I'll be able to stand the power of the orgasm he's forcing out of me. My fingers dig into the couch and scratch along his back.

He pulls away as my thighs loosen, and the sight of him is nearly enough that I cum just from looking at him. His chiseled frame is all ripped muscle, with his left arm covered in intricate tattoos. His eyes are intense with his own need, and his breath comes in pants. He stares at my pussy in awe as he curls his fingers and mercilessly rubs my G-spot. His thumb presses down on my clit and I find my body trying to turn away. It's too much. I can't stand the overwhelming sensation.

"Don't you move," he says while withdrawing his fingers. My eyes pop open and my breath finally comes back to me.

"I didn't mean to." I'm so ready. I want him so fucking bad. I was so close. So fucking close.

He smirks at me and backhands my clit. My back arches,

but my pussy clamps down on nothing. I need it. I'm so close.

"Bad girl," he says with a smirk. If he wasn't so fucking hot, and I wasn't so delirious with my own needs, I'd tell him off. Instead I bite my lip and wait with bated breath for him to take me over the edge. "Hold still." He lowers his head and relief flows through me, but it's immediately replaced with the tingling sensation of every inch of my skin being lit aflame.

He laps at my pussy, and gently places his thumb against my ass. My mouth opens as the foreign sensation of him pushing against me adds to the intensity of his tongue massaging my clit. My eyes close, and my lips part. My breathing comes in ragged pants as he starts fucking my ass and sucking my clit at the same time. It's too much. So fucking overwhelming.

In an instant, my body goes numb and then immediately explodes with paralyzing pleasure.

My thighs clench around his head as I cry out in complete ecstasy. Every nerve ending heats in waves, starting at my toes and working their way up. Each wave of pleasure is higher and more intense than the previous. My body is twisted and still stiff, unwilling to move. I try to relax as I come down from the high. I try, but my body doesn't respond. I can only feel.

After a few minutes of lying limp on the sofa, I come to my senses. My body is covered in sweat, and my legs are still trembling. I try to speak and realize my throat is sore and dry.

I look down my body and watch as Thomas stands up and shoves his jeans down his muscular thighs. He grabs his thick cock in his hands and strokes it once. The head glistens with a taste of his cum. He embodies power and lust. And the sight of him is intoxicating.

"I want you on the bed next." With the heated look in his eyes and my arousal glistening on his lips, I can't deny him. I can't deny what I want either. I love the way he makes me feel. In this moment I'd let him have me however he wanted. And I do.

I'll give him every bit of me that he wants.

I can't remember how long it's been since I've felt this alive. A spark I haven't felt in years is blazing inside of me. He lifts my body in his arms and carries me to the bedroom. I lean into him. I don't want to think about anything except how good it feels.

That's all I care about. I just want to *feel*.

He tosses me onto the bed and immediately crawls toward me. He looks dangerous, he *is* dangerous. He licks his lips and climbs over my body, forcing me onto my back.

His lips crush mine, and I can faintly taste myself on his tongue. I smile and pull back as a blush rises to my cheeks. His chest shakes gently with his rough chuckle, and it warms every bit of me.

"Where are your cuffs?" he asks. My eyes widen at his question. My heart races in my chest.

"You need to learn to trust me, baby." He kisses me with such passion I have to close my eyes.

"I can help you with that. Let me."

I pull away from him and look at my dresser. They're in the top drawer. My anxiety spikes.

"I can't." I push the words out. I know there's something between us, but what that is, I'm not sure.

"You can," he says, standing up from the bed. He walks to my dresser, following my line of sight and guessing correctly that the cuffs are there. They're right on top, so he doesn't have to look very long to find them.

"You could hurt me," I state simply. It's one thing to fool around, but another to give up control and make myself so helpless. I don't want to be vulnerable. The very thought chills my blood.

He looks at me with incredulity before pointing out, "My arm is almost as large as your head. I could hurt you right now if I wanted." My eyes linger on his corded arms and broad shoulders. I know what he's saying is true, but I don't like it. I don't like how accurate his words are.

"That right there," he walks back to me and gentles his hand on my forearm, "That fear. I'm going to take it away." I stare into his heated gaze and feel too much comfort.

"Why?" It's stupid to even consider it. But I am. I don't want to be scared anymore. I don't want to be angry, either.

He shrugs and dangles the two sets of cuffs from his finger. He watches as they sway. "You look like a girl who could use a little help."

"I don't need help." I know I sound defensive, and I don't mean to.

"No, you don't need it. But you could use it." He hands me the cuffs. "Lock them around your wrists." He gives me the command and it instantly heats my core. I have to stop myself from scissoring my legs.

"What are you going to do to me?" I ask him in a breathy voice. Now that I'm holding the cuffs in my hand and he's standing so close, it's turning me on. His muscular chest ripples as he takes a step back from me.

"I'm going to watch as you cuff yourself to the bed."

I bite my lip and watch him stroke himself. "Just the thought of you being at my mercy has me almost cumming. You know that?"

I feel my cheeks heat and a wave of arousal shoots through me. I shift the cuffs to my other hand and look at them and then at him.

"Then what?" I ask. My lips stay parted as my breathing comes in short pants.

"I'm gonna do whatever I want with you." My eyes fall and the insecurity comes back. I don't like not having a plan.

"I'm going to start by getting between your legs and getting your taste back on my tongue." My eyes shoot to his as I listen. "I need to get you ready to take me." My thighs clench, and I know I'm already ready.

"Not your pussy, baby. I want your ass." My eyes widen,

and I actually scoot away slightly on the bed. He chuckles and strokes himself again. My eyes focus on the bead of precum leaking from his slit.

"Not tonight, baby. But I'm gonna get you ready for me. Tonight I'm fucking your pussy like I own it. But next time, I'm taking your ass."

His words force a moan from my lips. I want that. I want all of that. But I don't want to give up control. I look up at him with apprehension, and see nothing but desire written on his face. I have to tell him how I really feel though. "I'm scared," I whisper, and it makes me feel weak.

"That's normal. But I promise you, you're going to love it."

"What if it's too much?" I ask.

He smirks at me as he says, "You have to trust me." He walks over and plants a soft kiss on my lips before I can object to anything else.

His hand strokes my hair. "All you need to do is trust me."

This is stupid and reckless, but I feel like I need this. I close my eyes and quickly tighten the cuffs on both my wrists. I bring my right hand up to the bedpost and attach the cuff to the thin metal cylinder.

My heart races in my chest. "Just tug, baby." I hear his words and it takes a second to understand the meaning of them. I do as he says. I pull against the restraint, and I can see why he wanted me to. If I struggle hard enough, the post will give. It'll fuck up my wrist, but I could get out. It would fucking hurt though.

"I won't do anything that'll make you feel like you need to. I just wanted you to realize, if you really needed to, you could take control back." He plants another soft kiss on my lips and I close my eyes and lie back against the pillow. I put my left wrist up against the post and wait for him to tighten it.

My heart races in my chest. He could do whatever he wants to me now. His grin widens into a gorgeous smile as his eyes roam my body.

"Spread your legs," he commands, and I instantly obey.

"See, you can be a good girl when you want to." He climbs on the bed and buries his head between my legs. I moan and arch my back as he sucks my clit into his mouth and massages it with his tongue. His fingers push into me and curl up, hitting the sensitive bundle of nerves. He's rough and brutal. His movements are harsh and strike my desire each and every time. My body heats so hot I swear I'm not alright and then the trembling waves start from the pleasure stirring in my center.

My orgasm hits me with a force I've never felt before. It comes so quickly, and so forcefully that I wasn't prepared. I scream and convulse as a white light blinds me and my skin turns to fire. He kisses my thigh, my hip. His rough stubble scratches gently across my sensitive skin and makes my body shudder.

I breathe heavily as I come back down and watch as he sucks on his fingers with a look of pure rapture.

He takes them out of his mouth with a pop and smirks at

me. "I told you you'd enjoy it. Now lie back and be a good girl for me. I'll give you everything you need."

When the morning light shines through the bit of my window not covered by the curtain, I roll over in my bed to avoid the light and reach out to nothing. My eyelids part and I sit up to make sure, but I already know he's gone. My hand rests where he was last night and it's cold.

I clench my thighs and feel so fucking sore. My pussy is slightly swollen and the movement sends a shot of need through me. If he was here, I'd want him again.

But he's not.

I lie on my back and stare at the ceiling not knowing how to feel, or what to think.

I want him, obviously, and our chemistry is undeniable, but I can't possibly expect anything to come of this. It's a bad idea to play a man who won't keep you. I pull the covers tighter around my shoulders and sink back into the warmth of the bed.

I close my eyes and try to ignore it. I'm not in any state to even think about what happened, let alone try to figure out where this is going.

Chapter 13

Tommy

I can't believe I'm here. I'm practically stalking a cop. She looks different today. She's wearing a cute little sundress. It's black on top, and white on the bottom, with a bright pink sash separating the two colors around her waist. It looks cute on her. Different, but cute. I watch as she takes off her sunglasses and looks into the window of a sandwich shop. She's hungry, good. I wanna feed her. I keep watching as she purses her lips and puts the sunglasses back on and walks closer to me, even though she's on the other side of the street and hasn't even seen me yet.

I'm just waiting for her to feel my eyes on her. I wanna see her reaction. I grin from ear to ear as she stops in her tracks with her head turned in my direction. A smile spreads across her gorgeous lips. That's a good reaction. I see her shoulders relax as she looks down the road, checking for oncoming traffic. She crosses the street and I motion for her to follow me into the shop I've been standing out in front of. I don't want us meeting on the street. We need to be inside for this.

Once I'm sure she knows I'm heading inside, I walk into the coffee shop and sit at a table near the back. No one should really notice us here. No one would recognize me so far from our territory. It's still a risk, but it's one I'm willing to take.

"What are you doing here?" she asks in a hushed voice as she sits down. She looks around the restaurant and I let her. I give her a moment to realize it's alright. Her hair is in a high ponytail, but a small piece has fallen out and it tickles along her collarbone. She turns to look at the customers in line. She looks so fucking beautiful. Her skin has a faint flush to it, and I'm not sure if it's because of me, or something else. But I'd love to think I caused it.

I wait for her to look at me with those beautiful green eyes full of curiosity. "I had nothing better to do."

"Nothing better than to follow me around?" Her tone has a bit of admonishment to it. But I know she's happy. I can tell. And I like that. Her hand is fiddling with the locket hanging from her necklace. I've seen her do that before. I wondered back then what's inside her locket, or who gave it to her. It's someone important and I want to find out, but now's not the time.

"Yeah, well, my day job is on hold at the moment." I watch her eyes widen as I answer her. She didn't expect me to talk about work, but if we're planning on fucking, and I sure as hell am, then we need to be blunt and honest.

She noticeably swallows and looks toward the front of the restaurant. "Should you really be telling me that?"

"Are you wired, baby? The last couple of times I've checked your clothes, you weren't." Her cheeks go bright red, and it's fucking adorable to see.

"Thomas--" I cut her off before she can finish.

"Tommy. Call me Tommy." It feels good telling her that. Such a stupid thing. But everyone calls me Tommy. And I want her to do the same. I shouldn't. I know this is wrong, but I do.

"Tommy, I don't know about this." I can hear the worry in her voice.

"What's there to know?" I shrug, and then lean in a little. "I like fucking you." My words make her smile even though she's trying to contain it. "I want what happened last night to happen again." Her chest rises and falls. Her pupils dilate with desire. I made sure to make up for the squeaky bed last night, and I know she enjoyed herself. I bet she can still feel me buried deep inside her.

"You know we shouldn't." Her words are breathy. I know I've got her. So long as I want her, she's mine.

My lips pull into an asymmetric grin as I agree, "Yeah, we shouldn't. But we're gonna. 'Cause I'm a bad boy, and you're a bad girl."

She bites her lip and rests her elbow on the table, cradling her cheek with her hand. Her forehead pinches with worry. "I don't know, Tommy."

"You don't know what? If you wanna cum on my dick again?"

As I ask the question, a barista walks up with a pad and pen to take our orders. I watch as Tonya's eyes go wide, and she looks down at her lap like there's something there that's going to save her from embarrassment. I doubt the barista heard because she seems unaffected, but that doesn't stop Tonya from having a moment.

"Can I get you two anything?" the girl asks in a sweet voice. She's young. If she heard, I doubt she'd be so calm.

"Yeah, could I have a coffee with cream, a blueberry muffin, a slice of banana nut bread..." I lean back to look at the menu. I figure I might as well order a few different things to see what Tonya likes. "A cake pop, and a cookie too, please."

"Is all that for you?" Tonya asks.

"I think I'll share with you." My answer makes her smile shyly. I like this side of her.

"Just a coffee, please. French Vanilla, with cream and sugar." She likes it sweet. I could've guessed that, but I wouldn't have been shocked if she liked her coffee black, too.

"So, what's it going to be, Tonya?" I ask as soon as the

waitress is out of sight.

She looks down at the table with pursed lips and then back up to me. "Just sex?" she asks.

"Yeah," I'm quick to answer.

My sweet forbidden bad girl. I want her so fucking bad.

"Okay," she agrees. My dick stands at full attention and pushes against my zipper. Yes! I can't fucking wait to be inside her again. It takes everything in me not to bend her over the table and fuck her right here and now.

I play it cool though, leaning back in my seat. "Good." I keep it simple and let my eyes wander to her breasts. I don't give a fuck that it's blatant. She's mine now. I remember biting down on her nipples and pulling back last night, forcing those moans from her lips. I can't fucking wait to do it again.

The barista sets a tray down in front of me, and brings me back to the present.

Tonya laughs under her breath and thanks the young girl before she walks away.

"I think you're drooling, Tommy," she says with confidence. She shoots me an I-own-your-ass type of look, and I fucking love it. I love how damn confident she is around me.

"I might be." I lift her hand to my mouth and make a sweet, soft giggle erupt from her lips. This side of her is different. It's soft and sweet. I like it. Even more, I like that I bring it out of her.

I watch her pick off the little bits of sugar on the top of

the muffin and pop them into her mouth. She picks at it for a while and then finally bites into it.

As she takes a bite, she looks up and sees me watching her. She's quick to cover her mouth as she chews and sets the muffin down. "What?" she asks, still covering her partially full mouth.

I chuckle at her and shake my head as I reply, "Nothing." It's cute I guess to watch her eat like that.

She finishes swallowing and takes a sip of coffee before asking me, "Aren't you going to eat?"

I shake my head. "No, I just thought you may be hungry."

She smiles sweetly and takes another sip of coffee. "I'm good to go, if you are. I have some errands to run." She wipes her hands on the napkin and tosses it onto her plate.

I nod my head and reach into my pocket for my wallet.

"You don't--" she starts, but I cut her off.

"Knock it off, I wanna buy you breakfast."

"Thank you," she looks shy as she says it. She downs the rest of her coffee and stands to leave.

"I'll walk you to your car." She looks at me for a moment, as though she doesn't understand. But as I stand she nods obediently. I might call her my bad girl, but she's so fucking good to me. She just doesn't know it.

Chapter 14

Tommy

As we walk out of the coffee shop, she looks all around us, like she's just waiting to be spotted. I don't know what the fuck is wrong with her. Apparently she forgot how to play it cool.

"Relax," I wrap my arm around her waist to make a point. "No one's gonna see us."

We walk in amiable silence. I let her lead the way.

After a few minutes she says, "I just don't know about this, Tommy." I hate the insecurity in her voice.

"You weren't concerned about that just a few minutes ago," I point out as I look down at her to watch her expression. "You changing your mind?"

"No, I--" she clears her throat and walks a bit straighter as she continues. "I enjoyed last night."

"Good, then there's no problem." I enjoyed it, too. I loved playing with her body. Watching how she responded to every move. I got her off every way I knew how. She was limp and sated and I still wanted more. I'll be damned if I'm not going to keep going after what I want. I've never known real limits before. I've never wanted to venture past what the *familia* gave me. But I'm not giving this up. Now that I've had a taste, I'm not willing to let go.

"This is just so wrong," she says as I spot her car. She parked behind a little shopping center. There are a few cars in front of us as we walk in, but hers is off to the side. It's a vacant lot. I take a quick glance to make sure no one's around us, and I decide right then that I'm gonna teach her a lesson.

She walks to her door but I take hold of her hip and keep her walking to the backseat door so we're a bit more hidden. She looks shocked and a little confused until I press my lips to hers, and let my hands roam down her body.

She breaks the kiss and looks out into the empty lot, seeming to remember we're out in public. That's the shit I'm gonna punish her for. Right fucking now.

"You wanna know how wrong it is?" I grab her ass in both my hands. I give her a firm squeeze that makes her gasp, and then spin her around in my arms. I shove her front against her car. Her breasts flatten against the window, making them appear even more lush and biteable. "You wanna see how much I don't give a fuck that it's wrong?"

My hand cups her pussy and I have to stifle my groan. She's already hot and wet and ready for me. I've waited long enough for that ass, though. I push the inside of her thigh and she obliges, spreading her legs. She looks over her shoulder to look at me with a wicked spark in her eyes and taunts, "You gonna punish me?" Those words on her lips nearly has me cumming in my pants.

I'm quick to unzip my pants and unleash my cock. I stroke it once as her mouth opens and her tongue darts out to lick her bottom lip. She looks around the parking lot like there's no way we aren't getting caught. I almost change up my plans and push her down onto her knees to have her suck me off, but this isn't about me taking pleasure from her. It's about her seeing just how much we can get away with.

"Only if you're quiet." I grip the nape of her neck and pull her back so I can take her bottom lip between my teeth. Her ass backs up against my cock and she teases me, rocking it back and forth like she wants to ride me.

I let go of her and lift up her dress. The desire written on her face fades as she hears voices coming through the narrow sidewalk. She looks at me with a hint of fear. I hold her gaze as the voices fade just as quickly as they came. I'm sure these cars belong to employees of these shops. No one's coming back here. I know she's scared of getting caught. I'm gonna show her that shit's not going to happen.

"Your greedy pussy wants me, but you're gonna have to wait." My thumb probes her puckered hole, and the motion makes her moan. A rough chuckle grows up my chest as I slip on a lubricated condom. I hate condoms, but for this I need to make sure there's lube. She's gonna need it. I spit in my hand and make sure my dick is nice and wet for her. I line my cock up and slowly push just the head in. I gotta get her loose and feeling good before I finally take her ass with my dick. I've been thinking about it all day.

"Tommy," she moans my name as my fingers dip inside her heat and spread her moisture to her swollen clit. I pinch her lightly and she arches her back in response, causing my dick to slip in a little deeper. It feels so fucking good. I wanna slam into her, but this is the first time, I've gotta be gentle.

My arm wraps around the front of her so I can cup her pussy. I press my palm to her clit and gently slip my fingers into her hot cunt. I rock my hand as I pick up my motions. I keep rubbing her clit and playing with her pussy until she writhing under my touch and letting her moans slip out with no inhibition.

She's getting louder and bolder, moving her pussy against my hand to take what she wants. That's exactly how I need her. She's so fucking easy to get off. A few more rough pumps and she's biting down on her lip while her thighs tremble with her orgasm. Her pussy clamps down on my fingers and I'm too fucking excited to get my pleasure next.

"You like that, baby?" I ask her.

She tilts her head slightly and smirks as she answers, "Fuck you, you know I do." I fucking love it. I love how she pushes me.

I put my lips up to her ear and speak in a low, threatening voice. "My bad girl is really pushing it. That's a brave thing for you to do with my dick in your ass."

I take a quick look up and to my left. I've been so busy watching her I haven't been paying attention, but there's no one there.

Soon she'll be ready for me to fuck her rough and deep. I just need a few more minutes to get her ready. I keep looking ahead of us and every voice makes my heart beat a little faster. She's trusting me, and I don't want to ruin it because I was so damn set on fucking her ass.

I aim my spit and get my cock more lubed as I push in a bit more and pull out. "Push back, baby," I tell her.

She obeys me and I slide in a little deeper. It only takes a few more gentle rocks until she's moaning and pushing back to take more of me.

Finally, I'm all the way in, and it feels like fucking heaven. She moans against the window, and I take a quick look to make sure no one can see her. Right now she's mine. I pull out slowly and push back in with just as much care. I need to be gentle until she's adjusted to me being inside her.

Her forehead pinches, and I know she's feeling a little

pain. I rub her clit to make sure it's only going to heighten her pleasure. I don't want to hurt her. I want this to be just as good for her as it is for me. Each movement makes those sweet sounds fall from her lips. Her eyes are closed, and her hands are gripping onto the frame of her car. She's completely lost in pleasure.

"Tommy," she whispers my name. "Harder, fuck me harder." Her words are a desperate plea.

I grip her hips and thrust into her harder. She cries out, and I have to wrap my hand around her mouth. I lean in and growl into her ear. "You want everyone to see me fucking you, don't you?"

She shakes her head and moans into my hand as I keep fucking her ass like I own her. My balls smack against her pussy with each hard thrust. Over and over I pound into her. She struggles to keep quiet, and I have to remind her. "Shut the fuck up and take it." Her pussy clamps down on my fingers at my dirty words. She's loving this. I move my other hand away from her mouth so I can grip her hip and mercilessly fuck her ass. She bites her lip and pushes her head and breasts against the car door.

"Where's my cock, baby?" I ask her as I keep up my ruthless rhythm. Her ass is tight and hot, and I'm getting close already.

"In my ass," she whimpers, and her mouth stays open with her eyes closed tight. I know she's close again. She just needs a little more.

"That's 'cause you're a bad girl, and bad girls get fucked in their ass." I thrust in and out of her, loving the soft moans she's giving me. I strum her clit as she pushes back against me. "Do you feel like a bad girl now?" My body starts to sweat, and my breathing gets labored as I give her ass a punishing fuck.

"Yes." She's louder than she should be, and it makes my eyes dart up. Still no one.

"Say it." I push my dick all the way in and lift my hips so I'm as deep as I can go. Her mouth opens in a silent scream. I pull back slightly, and she's quick to obey my command.

"I'm your bad girl." Her words bring me that much closer to my release, and I desperately rub her throbbing clit to get her off. I need her cumming with me. Her body goes limp, and her legs tremble. Her head flies back with her teeth digging into her bottom lip. Fuck yes. I pump into her again, and fucking lose it. I hear her words over and over in my head as my spine tingles and waves of pleasure rush through my body. I thrust my hips once more to give her everything I've got.

I pull out of her gently and steady her hips. Her legs are quivering, and I know she must feel weak. She took a rough fuck. "Lean against the car, baby. I got you." She listens and rests her head on the window, catching her breath. I look to my left and right, and there's still no one there. Thank fuck. I don't want anyone to see her like this.

I remove the condom and tuck my dick back in my pants.

She's still trying to regain her composure, so I pull her panties back into place as her breathing calms. I pet her back in soothing circles. Her hair has fallen out, and I have to push it away to give her a small kiss on her shoulder.

After a minute she rolls her body on the car so that her back is leaning against it and she's facing me. She gives me a small, satisfied smile and it fills my chest with pride. I knew she'd like that. I give her a kiss just below the tender spot behind her ear. She hums with approval. My lips tickle her neck as I ask her, "Did you like that, bad girl?"

"You fucked the ponytail out of my hair," she says weakly, with a bit of humor. Her eyes light with happiness, and the smile grows on her gorgeous face.

I shrug and wrap an arm around her waist as she bends down with trembling legs to pick up the hair tie on the ground. She looks around us as she stands up. "Did anyone see?" she asks with a quiet voice.

"Not this time." I grin at her.

She gives me a small smile, but I can see she doesn't like that answer. She runs her fingers through her hair and breathes deeply. "Just sex." She says it like it's a reminder. To herself and to me.

She takes a few steps to her door, looking as though nothing even happened. She's pulled herself together, the only signs that she just took my cock up her ass are the flush in her cheeks, and her slightly swollen bottom lip.

I clear my throat and answer her, "Yeah, just sex." That's all this is. I'm fine with that. And she sure as shit enjoys it just as much as me.

She nods and steps out of my embrace to open her door.

"I have to get going." Her words are weak, almost filled with regret.

"Yeah, me too." No I don't. I don't have shit to do but fuck her. Even though she's the one that's supposed to be watching me, so I could probably run errands. It'd be stupid to risk it though.

She parts her lips and looks up at me through her lashes as she settles into the driver side door. She winces slightly instead of saying whatever was on her mind. I don't know what she was going to say, but she decides on nothing. It makes an uneasiness settle in my chest. She's unsure of something.

"You good?" I try to keep it lighthearted, but she just nods and doesn't look me in the eyes.

"I'll see you later," I tell her. I lean in and plant a small kiss on her cheek.

"Okay," she says, looking up at me with a slightly confused look. I don't understand where it's coming from.

"You alright?" I ask her.

"Yeah, I'm good," she says as she puts the key into the ignition. But she's not good. I don't like it.

I want to ask her why she's being so distant, but I hold back. No questions is better. For both of us. I wanna fuck her, she wants to fuck me, we have to leave it at that. I grip her doorframe and gently close it as she lowers the window.

"I'll see you later then," she says, and I give her a tight smile.

As she drives away, I can't help but feel like I'm not going to see her again. She's going to realize what a mistake this is.

I want to prove to her it's not, but it is. Maybe I should just stay away. I run my hand through my hair and sigh. I don't know what I was thinking. It's gonna be like this every time we leave each other. And I don't like this raw hollowness in my chest.

I watch her car drive away before I start walking back through the opening to the sidewalk.

I hate how she left. But that's what this is. It's all it can be.

It didn't occur to me that I don't just want sex until right this moment. And that's not good. That's not fucking good at all.

Fuck, this was a mistake. A big, fucking mistake.

CHAPTER 15

TONYA

I stare at the folders on my desk, and then back up at the computer screen. I have a ton of shit to update. I need to put all this information in the system, but I keep fucking up. I have to do this right, but my head's not in it. I just can't think straight. I'm exhausted from the last two days on the job. I'm miserable.

It's not that the work is any harder, it's just not what I want to do.

I'm on cases that mean nothing to me. I'm getting spit on and kicked while I arrest assholes I don't give a shit about. I feel beat up and abused. I know this is the right thing to do and people do appreciate it, even if I never hear it. But damn, this is hard. And it's wearing me down.

I heard back from our contacts in France and Russia, still no sign of Petrov. He has to be dead.

I feel defeated more than anything. Like the finish line vanished before I could make it there.

"How's it coming along?" Chris' voice makes me jump in my seat. He laughs at me and pats my back. "You need more coffee."

I smile weakly up at him. Chris has been a cop all his life. He's gotta be in his fifties now, but he's still smiling, and still kicking ass. I don't know how he does it.

He's not chasing a case or running toward the darkness. He deserves to be a cop. I don't. I was using this position for my own selfish reasons. I feel like fraud.

"Yeah, for real." I clear my throat and scoot back in my seat. "I'll run out and grab one, you want anything?"

"Nah, I'm good," he says. "Hey, I just wanna say, you're doing good, kid. Don't be so hard on yourself."

"Thanks." I try to look him in the eyes, but I can't.

"We can't get 'em all, and the Valettis are a big fish. It'll go on their file, so we can use it next time. Trust me, there will be a next time."

I look up at him with a deep crease of confusion marring my forehead. "What are you talking about?"

"Oh shit. I thought you were all bent out of shape because the prosecutor gave you the news."

"No, Marcy didn't tell me shit."

"Fuck, she must've told Harrison. He didn't tell you? He's

supposed to be taking you under his wing."

I huff a humorless laugh. "No, he didn't."

"The judge ruled against us. We can't use the fingerprints." He shrugs and looks like he feels guilty for telling me. "There's no case." I don't answer. I don't know what to say.

"He really should've told you."

A lump grows in my throat. Tommy's off the hook.

He's going to be okay. A weight lifts from my chest, but that only makes the pain I'm feeling there grow stronger.

"You okay?" Chris asks. I look at him for a moment. I see the kindness in his eyes, and I know I don't deserve it.

"Yeah, I'm--"

"Kelly! We need to talk." Harrison interrupts us, and I swear to God I'm gonna strangle him if he yells at me.

"Yeah, I'm all ears," I say, not holding back the sarcasm.

"We lost our case, but I'm betting something's gonna blow up in their faces soon. We just gotta stay the course."

I'm surprised by his tone. It's not condescending or full of anger. He's almost excited.

"Why do you think it's going to blow back on them?"

"You can't fuck over a Kingpin and not get dealt with."

"I imagine Petrov is dead," I say flatly. It kills me to say it, but it's the truth.

"Possibly, but Nikolaev has taken over." He says the words like Petrov was no one special. After a moment of quiet he adds, "There's always going to be another one."

My heart thuds once in my chest and stops. I try to push the words out, but I can't hear them.

"You've got a lot to learn." He grins at me. "We're gonna get 'em. I know we will. They're getting sloppy, and soon enough, it's gonna happen." I've never seen him this happy and I don't know how to handle him. Or all the emotions bombarding me.

He pats me on the back and turns to walk away. "I can *feel* it. It's coming," he says as he walks off.

I try to sit back down, but I can't. I just need to get out of here. Something in my gut is telling me everything is wrong. And it's all revolving around Tommy.

It's been four days since I've seen him. I don't understand. I thought he meant he'd see me later that night. But he never showed. I guess I was presumptuous. And then I got a message. A text from his cell. I only know because I looked up the number.

I'm sorry, Tonya. It's over. You were right.

He told me to stay away. It fucking hurt.

I know it was wrong. I knew we shouldn't have done it. But still. It was nice to be held. I feel like I have nothing. I have no one. I need something. I need *him* right now. Whether he wants me or not. That's my selfish side coming through again. I wonder if I'll ever learn.

I take a deep breath and grab my jacket to get out of here. I walk over to Jerry's office, but stop before knocking. The door's ajar, and I can hear him talking to his wife on the phone. I press my lips into a straight line as I listen to him lie to her about being on a job last night. I take a peek at him and see he's still in his clothes from yesterday. My heart drops in my chest.

It hurts to think he's cheating on her, but it's so fucking obvious. I don't ask to leave early, I just keep walking and try to ignore all this shit. My thoughts are running a mile a minute, about everything, and everyone. I thought I had shit all figured out, but I didn't.

I don't have anything figured out. I'm just lost. I'm so fucking lost.

I thought I knew how all of this would play out, but now what I wanted seems impossible.

I thought I knew what Tommy would be like before I ever met him. I read his profile and looked at the evidence. I had him painted in my head as an arrogant prick who thought he could get away with whatever he wanted. And then I met one of the women. The only one who was coherent. She said she saw Tommy. She heard gunshots and shouting, but she couldn't move. She wasn't sure if it was the drugs or the fear. She was in and out of it for a while, but one of them, one of the Valettis shot her up with something. She tried to make him stop, like the other times. But they said it was to make her better. To help save her. And it did. And Tommy was the one calming her down and telling her it would be okay.

My heart clenches in my chest. The line between black and white is so goddamned blurry. And at this point, I'm having a hard time knowing what's right and what's wrong.

Chapter 16

Tommy

I look out of the peephole and my heart sinks. I knew this was going to happen. I'm surprised she waited. I prepared for her anger that night when I sent the text. It's not fucking right the way I ended it. I rest my head on the door and she knocks again. Right in that very spot. Like she fucking knew I was there.

It hurts, and I wince like a little bitch. Shit! I need to get this over with. I open the door and part my lips to tell her I'm sorry, but she walks right past me, brushing against my body and continuing to the bedroom like I wasn't even standing in the doorway.

What the fuck?

"Tonya!" I call after her, but she doesn't stop. I shut the door and follow her to my bedroom, not knowing what to expect.

I walk in and find her sitting on the edge of my bed, waiting for me. She's gripping the edge of the comforter and looking at the ground.

"Charges are dropped," she says to the floor.

I take in her appearance. She's nothing like the woman I was with this past weekend. Not the sweet spitfire in a sundress. She's hurting bad. I walk over and sit next to her on the bed, but I keep my hands to myself. We can't keep this shit up.

"I know." I'm not going to tell her I found out from the judge. She doesn't ask though. She's quiet for a while. I let her sit and think. I won't push her to tell me why she's here.

"I need you right now, Tommy," she finally says. Tears leak from the corners of her eyes and it breaks my heart in two. I lose my resolve and wrap her small body in my arms. I pull her into my lap and hold her while she cries.

"What's wrong, baby?" She cries harder at my words, and I can't stand it. I just want her to stop. She's a strong woman. I didn't think I'd hurt her like this. "I'm sorry." I kiss her neck. I wish there were another way. I wish we hadn't met like this. "I'm sorry it has to be this way."

She nods her head into my chest, but she doesn't let up on the tears. I stroke her back and rock her. Kissing her hair, her shoulder. I keep soothing her the best I can.

"You don't deserve this, baby. You deserve better."

She shakes her head and heaves in a shaky breath. "Don't

act like I'm good enough for you. I'm not. I'm a thug, and you're a cop," I point out.

She doesn't respond. The only reaction I get is that her cries slowly stop. It takes a few more minutes before she lifts her head and wipes away the tears.

Her cheeks are tear-stained and red, her eyes are glassy. She sniffles and I reach to the nightstand for a tissue for her.

"You're gonna be alright, babe, you're going places." My heart clenches in my chest. I don't wanna do this. I have to admit, when she didn't come that night it hurt, even though I told her to stay away. A part of me hoped she wouldn't listen, and she'd come to me. Even if it was just to yell at me for putting her through that shit. But I realized it was for the best. I'm only gonna hold her back. I'll ruin her career. And just being with me puts both of us in danger with the *familia*. It's impossible.

She was right to question us being together. It never should've happened.

"I just need to feel something right now." She turns her head to look at me. Her eyes are pleading with me. And I sure as hell am not going to refuse her. I want her. Even if it's only once more.

"I'm here." I pull her into my chest and lie on my side to cradle her. I leave an opened-mouth kiss on her neck. She takes my face in both of her hands and crushes her lips against mine.

I can feel all of her emotion pouring into her kiss. She

needs me right now. I can't deny her anything. In this moment, I'm only hers. She takes my bottom lip between hers and kisses me sweetly. I moan into her mouth as she parts her lips and grants me entry. My hand brushes against her hip and then slowly lifts her shirt. I let my fingers skim her skin. I smile against her lips as she pulls away and shivers from my touch.

I lift her shirt over her head. I kiss her belly, her breasts, and then the dip in her throat. I can hear her heart beating calmly as she raises her hands above her head. The tie holding up her hair loosens and slips out, letting her hair fall around her shoulders. She shakes it out gently and looks back at me with her beautiful green eyes. There's a small amount of lust and desire, but mostly need and vulnerability.

My heart swells in my chest as I grip her hips to keep her steady and lean forward, making her fall back on the bed as I kiss her. I suck her top lip and move down her body. I kiss her belly as I unbutton her jeans and slide them off. I watch as the goosebumps slowly show along her skin. My hot breath blows across her skin as my fingers slip off her thong and leave her completely bared to me.

I've never felt so powerful as I do when I look down at her. It feels like a heavy weight on my shoulders, but I want it. I want her. I want to give her everything she needs.

I take a languid lick as her fingers spear through my hair. Her thighs tremble as I blow over her sensitive clit.

"Please, Tommy," she moans into the air above me. I look up and find her staring down at me. "I need you," she whispers.

I kick off my pants and crawl up her body. I kiss her once and watch as her eyes close while I slowly push into her. I lower my head and groan into the crook of her neck as her back bows, and I slide deeper inside of her welcoming heat. I angle my hips so I push against her clit as I settle in as deep as I can go.

I brace myself on my forearms, and watch as her mouth parts with small pants and her eyes stay closed. I cup her chin in my hand and lean down for a sweet kiss. I give her a moment to adjust to my size, and then I pull back and slam into her. Her eyes open as she gasps from the impact and pleasure.

I hold her gaze as I do the same again and again, hitting her clit each time.

"More," she whispers. I run my hand over her thigh and let my blunt fingernails dig into her ass. I tilt her so she's at just the right angle and hold her there as I thrust harder and deeper. Her head rocks, and her breasts bounce slightly with each pump of my hips, but her eyes stay on mine.

I want to kiss her, I want to bury my head into her neck and fuck her with wild abandon, but I can't. I can't break her gaze. I pick up my pace and brutally fuck into her greedy cunt, again and again. A strangled cry of pleasure escapes her lips as her thighs tremble and her nails dig into my back, leaving small scratches behind. I feel her walls tighten and I know she's close. She's so close, and so am I.

I suck her nipple into my mouth and pull back. My teeth bite down enough to hold on as I pull back. Her back bows off the bed as I do the same to the other breast. My breathing comes in pants and so does hers. It's all I can hear. It's all that matters right now.

I pick up my pace and gently kiss her lips. It's soft, and our lips barely touched, but it feels like more. Her lips stay parted as she moans my name. "Please, please," she keeps begging me, and I thrust harder and deeper every time, but I know this isn't what she's begging for. It only fuels me to hold her closer and kiss her more deeply, searching for the same feeling. I give her everything I have.

Her body tries to twist away beneath me as she calls out my name. *My name*. It sounds perfect coming from her lips. I slip my hands under her knees and push them forward. Her head thrashes as I fuck deep into her pussy. My hips smack against hers with each brutal thrust. Faster and harder until I can feel the highest peak. It's so close.

"Tommy!" she cries out as her body shakes uncontrollably. My name on her lips. I'll never stop loving that. It just sounds too perfect.

My spine tingles at the base, and a cold sweat breaks out over my entire body as I pump into her three more times, chasing that high that I always get with her. And then her eyes close, and her body trembles beneath me with her own orgasm. I find my release with her, lowering my head to her neck and breathing in her sweet scent.

After a moment, when the high of our release dies, the pounding need of my heart slows, and I realize it's over.

That was the last time.

Chapter 17

Tommy

I know when I let go, I'll never hold her again. She's lying still in my arms, thinking the same, I'm sure.

So I don't move. I pretend there's no reason for her to leave my embrace. That there's nothing waiting for either of us beyond these walls.

But I'm weak. I'm the weaker of the two of us, because she's the first to speak.

"Thank you," she murmurs without looking at me. She's thanking me, like I did her a favor. Like she didn't feel that. She didn't feel the same emotions I felt between us. I rest my head just above hers on the pillow.

"Don't thank me. Don't degrade what just happened like

that." The words come out harsher than I intended.

Her shoulders turn inward like she's cowering from my hard words. I wanna tell her I love her. But it'll only make it harder. After a minute, she molds her body against me again and relaxes in my embrace. I kiss her hair, and just as I lose my resolve and decide I should risk it all and tell her, I hear my front door open.

My blood turns to ice. I move quickly to get to the other side of Tonya, to block her from whoever just came into my place uninvited. A million possibilities race through my mind. It could be the cops coming to get me for something, a rival prick trying to prove he's tougher than me. For all I know, I could be on someone's hit list. I open my drawer for my gun. But then I hear Anthony's voice as he calls out, "Tommy! Where are you, bro?" My heart only races faster as I look between Tonya and the closed bedroom door.

"Wait here," I whisper to Tonya as she stares at the closed door with fear.

"Coming!" I yell out to him before leaning down and kissing her.

"Yo! We gotta talk!" I hear Anthony yell, and I resist the urge to hold her longer and finally back away.

I grab my pants and shove them on as quick as I can. I can't let him back here. I can't let him see her.

By the time I get to my living room, I'm pissed and aggravated. And worried. I breathe out slowly as I see Anthony going through the liquor cabinet. He turns to face me with two glasses in one hand, and a bottle of scotch in the other.

"What's wrong? You're all good now. Why the fuck do you look like that?" Anthony's pissing me off, but it's not his fault. I gotta calm down, but I can't. My heart's banging in my chest with the fear that shit's about to get real.

"I'm fine. What's up?" I ask him flatly.

"You don't look fine," he says.

I exhale heavily and think of a way to get him out of here.

"We gotta talk about Judge Steckel. He wants his--"

I'm quick to cut him off. I know she can hear, and this shit cannot fucking happen right now. "Not now, I can't talk now."

He looks at me like I'm fucked in the head. And he's right, too, 'cause I am fucked.

"You can't talk to me?" he asks.

"Not at the moment." His eyes fly to the bedroom.

He looks confused for a moment, and then it hits him. "Are you serious, she's back there?" His arms lower and he almost drops everything in his hands. "You've gotta be fucking kidding me."

Tonya must've heard him because she comes out, pulling her shirt down and looking all sorts of pissed and upset.

"You're a fucking idiot, Tommy." Anthony sneers his words and moves to the other side of the room while she walks to the door. He intentionally turns his back to her, snubbing her, and it's the last straw.

"What the fuck is wrong with you? Don't treat her like that!" I grab his shoulder and turn him around to face me while Tonya walks past us.

"Like what? Like a cop?" He raises his voice with disgust as I hear the door open.

"You're a fucking prick." I turn away from him. I have nothing to say, and I need to get to Tonya before she leaves.

"Me?!" he yells with disbelief. He grabs my arm to stop me from going to her and I turn around and swing. I don't hold back and hit him square in the jaw.

His back hits the wall and leaves a dent in the drywall from his right shoulder and head. He winces from the pain and cradles his chin. I feel regret for only a second. But he crossed the line.

He looks up at me with raw anger in his eyes. He spits blood onto my floor and rights himself. I face him, waiting for his response, waiting for something.

He flexes his jaw and avoids eye contact. "I have to tell him," he finally says with a hard look. His eyes flash with pity, anger, and betrayal.

"You know I'm not saying shit to her." My heart beats wildly in my chest.

"I can't fucking believe this, Tommy. What have you done?" His voice cracks on the last word.

"I just wanted her." That's all this is. We just wanted each other. We fit together in some crazy, fucked up way.

"You wanna get laid, you go to the strip joint." He looks at me with a pained expression. "You had to settle on a cop?"

"It didn't happen like that." He doesn't understand.

"Fuck, Tommy." He leans back against the wall as I look to the door.

"I have to go get her," I tell him, feeling like I'm stabbing him in the back.

"How could you even think it's gonna be alright?" he asks.

"It's not, I know it's not. It's over, she just needed me."

He snorts a laugh as he sarcastically says, "Yeah, I'm sure she needed you."

"One warning, Anthony." I walk toward him and hold his stare. "Don't talk about her like that."

He holds my gaze for a moment, neither one of us backing down. And then I break it and grab my keys.

"Tommy, just think about what you're doing," he calls out after me.

I look back at him over my shoulder, with my hand on the doorknob.

I'm betraying the *familia*. I'm risking everything. But I can't let it end like this.

I hit the gas pedal on the way to her place. She got a head start, but I wanna get there before she has a chance to think too much. If Anthony hadn't barged in there, I don't know what would've happened, but something was happening. I know we need to end this. But I don't want to hurt her. She said she needed me, and I owe it to her to at least make sure she's okay.

As I pull in front of her place, I see her car and she's sitting in it, with her head down. Her hands are covering her face, and her shoulders are shaking. She's crying. The realization makes my heart sink.

I pull in a few cars down and quickly make my way to her as she opens her door. She stands up and goes still when she sees me. Her face is red, and her eyes are swollen. I don't waste any time pulling her into my chest and hugging her. At first she's tense and stiff in my arms, but I know she'll relax. What we have between us is fucked up, but I know I make her feel good. Just like she does for me.

She molds to me and I don't hold back, leaving little kisses on her cheek and neck and shoulder.

"I'm sorry," I tell her. I don't know what else to say.

She shakes her head and sadly says, "Don't be." She wipes under her eyes and pulls away from me. "You were right to end it. This shouldn't be happening. I shouldn't have come to you."

She pushes away slightly, and I almost let her, but instead I tighten my grip on her.

"One more night, Tonya. Just one night more."

She stares at me with longing in her eyes before saying, "When I wake up, Tommy, you can't be there." The finality is evident in her voice. Her hand cups my chin, and her eyes water. I nod my head and kiss the palm of her hand and lean into her touch. It hurts like a bitch, but I answer her, "I know. I'll be gone."

Chapter 18

Tommy

I don't know what to expect as I walk up to Aunt Linda's. I know Vince knows. Anthony called to apologize and told me he wouldn't say shit. But I told him to. If anything happens, I don't want the *familia* thinking Anthony knew something, but didn't say anything. I know fucking around with Tonya wasn't smart. I'm going to have to take the consequences. I just don't know what they'll be.

I grip the doorknob and push the door open. The normal sounds of Sunday dinner fill the air. Gino and Jax are running around the living room making screeching tire noises. The women are in there chatting away and bouncing the kids on their knees like the shrill noise is normal.

I'm already starting to get a headache. I walk past them giving a short wave and head to the right, to the dining room. Most of the family is already here. Looks like I'm the last to arrive. Uncle Dante sees me and smiles. The guys carry on with their conversation. Everything seems normal. It's not quite what I expected. I anticipated Vince laying a punch on me the second he saw me, but instead he keeps talking and gives me a nod to let me know he's there.

"Tommy!" Aunt Linda comes up behind me and gives me a hug even though she's got an oven mitt on one of her hands. She plants a kiss on my cheek and says, "You got here just in time. Dinner's almost ready."

I chuckle at her as she keeps on moving to the kitchen, "Dinner's always *almost* ready," I tease.

She smiles over her shoulder, but keeps moving. I take a seat at the table and listen in as Dom rattles off some numbers and argues with Joey about a college football game. If I had to guess, I'd bet Joey made a dumb bet. And judging by Dom's smile, that bet was with him.

"Anthony." Vince calls out my name, but so quietly, only I hear him. The rest of the conversation carries on around us as I look at him down the table.

"Yeah?" I ask.

"Help me with something outside real quick. I gotta carry this painting shit to the car for Elle." I stand up and follow him out. No one seems to notice.

My heart beats a little faster as we walk out front. This is it. I take a deep breath. I went against orders. I fucked around with a cop. Shit could get real ugly, and I'd fucking deserve it.

"Anthony told me what was going on," Vince says as we stand out on the porch.

"Yeah, I know."

"How long?" he asks.

"Not long. It's only been a few times."

"A few times is a few times too many." He lowers his voice and he leans into me as he says, "You lied to my face."

"I didn't." I shake my head. "I never lied to you." I would've told him if he'd asked. "Things got carried away." He steps back with a real pissed-off expression, and I put my hands up in surrender.

"I fucked up. I know that, Vince. It wasn't supposed to happen."

"A cop though, Tommy, what the fuck? I told you to stay away." The anger he's feeling at me comes out in his voice.

"I know. I--" He cuts me off before I can finish.

"You can fuck any broad you want, Tommy. You got 'em hanging all over your dick at the club. Why would you settle for a fucking cop? One I told you I wanted you to stay the fuck away from."

I look away, not liking how he's talking to me. I also don't like the way he's talking about Tonya. Like her being a cop is such a bad thing. She's good at keeping her mouth shut. She trusts me. It could've worked. Even though we're done with, I find myself defending her. "We have judges in our back pocket. Why not a cop?"

"She could never be with you if we had her on our payroll. It doesn't work like that. Red fucking flags everywhere, Tommy. The whole point is for us to stay far away from those people. So there's no goddamn connection."

"I'm sorry, Vince. She didn't get anything from me," I tell him.

"She could've though. You let a cop get close to you. That looks real fucking bad."

"It doesn't matter, Vince. It's over."

"You're damn right it's over. I have no fucking clue what to do with you." He runs his hands through his hair and starts pacing. "If you were anyone else, you'd be dead. You know that?"

His bold statement makes the air leave my lungs. I do know. I knew it was stupid, and it was risky. But he's gotta know I'd never say shit.

"And thank fuck it was your brother who saw. If it was someone else...If anyone else knew?" He shakes his head but his eyes aren't angry anymore. Now he just looks sad as fuck. "Don't you fucking put me in that position."

"I won't. It's over." I say the words with a defeated tone. Any thought of going back to her is gone. If they'd kill me, I know they'd get rid of her, too. I can't risk that.

"It's over, over. It's completely done with?" he asks.

"Yeah, it never should've happened." My heart twists in my chest as I say the words. He wraps his arm around my shoulder and pats my back.

"Thank fuck, Tommy." He walks us back inside and we stand in the foyer. Aunt Linda is setting dishes down on the table and Elle's strapping Angelo into his highchair.

Vince lowers his voice and reminds me, "No one can know about this. You know that, right?"

"Of course I know." I nod my head as I watch the scene in front of me unfold as though I'm not even there.

I watch in a daze as Elle sings in an upbeat voice to Angelo. "Sitting in my high chair, my chair, high chair. Sitting in my high chair, banging my spoon!" She bangs on the tray in rhythm to the words, and the little one squeals with joy.

Vince is saying something, but all I can hear is Elle. The happiness in her voice, the love in her words. I want Tonya to have that. She deserves that. I could give it to her. I should go to her and beg for her to take me back. I'd give her the world. I'd change for her. I swear I would.

She asked me for one thing, and I never even gave it to her. All this time I could've told her. I should've told her that Petrov's dead. But I didn't.

"Jesus, Tommy! Are you even listening to me?" Vince's voice snaps me out of it and I turn to look at him. I feel all choked up like a little bitch.

"You gotta get your shit together," he says.

"Yeah, I know, boss."

"I'm talking to you as family, Tommy. What the fuck is wrong with you? You should be happy. The charges were dropped. You're a free man, but you look like death."

I shake my head, not knowing how to tell him. I look back at my cousin and know that I can't. You don't leave the *familia*. Well, there's one way to leave.

I turn my head back to Elle as Vince leaves me with a pissed-off sigh.

"Bring on the carrots, bring on the peas," she lowers her voice, "Somebody feed this baby, please."

Both she and her baby laugh. My eyes drop to the floor.

I don't deserve Tonya. I won't ever be able to give her that. I'm only going to bring her more pain or worse...

Chapter 19

Tonya

I feel like hell, I look like hell; I'm fucking living in hell. I'm in a meeting with half a dozen cops going over the portfolio of several suspects in the investigation. There have been three reports of missing women in the upper east side suburb over the last two months, all fitting the same description.

I can't even look at their pictures. Melissa was a tall blonde with dark brown eyes. These women look nothing like her. Yet I only see her face. She's staring back at me. And I can't face her. I have nothing. I've come this far, for nothing.

"I wish we'd known when the other women were abducted." For some reason I blurt out the words, and Harrison pauses his presentation.

"Which women?" Jerry asks from my left. "All their data is in the portfolio."

I shake my head. "The twelve. Petrov's dozen." That's what they named them at the station. It's what the media used when they released the story. I hate it. I hate the name. Each woman was her own person, with her own name. But that's how they're referred to here. And I've been trying the 'fake it till you make it' approach. So I'll do what's expected and call them that. But I hate it.

"What do you mean? We knew," Carl answers from across the table. He's an officer like me, with a few years of experience under his belt. But a nice guy in general. He's got a wife and two kids. One's in middle school and the other is in kindergarten. I stare at him blankly, thinking I must've heard wrong. We didn't know Petrov's men had them. We had eyes on two locations. We were waiting for him to be seen so we could arrest him. We had enough against the other men, three were wanted in multiple countries. We left them as bait for Petrov. But we didn't know about the women until the day we found them.

"You were a bit wet behind the ears, so you weren't in on that intel, but we had eyes on a Felipe Barros."

Harrison continues for Carl, and I look between the two of them with a mixture of disbelief, hate, and disgust. "It was important that we waited until Petrov was spotted so that we could link him to the abductions."

"You knew where the women were located?" I ask in a voice I don't recognize. It's almost like I'm watching the scene, rather than participating.

Jerry puts his hand on my forearm in an attempt to placate me, but I pull away and stare at him. "We felt it was best since you were new on the case to keep you in the dark on some aspects. We were planning on telling you, but everything just happened so fast."

They knew. I look around the table and everyone's eyes are on me.

"You all knew?"

"Not about all of them. We had reason to believe that three of the women were being held at their headquarters," Harrison says.

"But you didn't go in?" I look at him with confusion.

"We couldn't risk the operation," Harrison responds simply.

"But we could've saved them."

"We did." Harrison speaks up and I find myself biting my tongue. *We* didn't save anyone.

"What about Georgia Stevens?" I ask them with a dull voice.

"Which one is that?" Carl asks. My eyes bore into his skull.

"She was the victim in Abram's car," Jerry answers to my left. I clench my teeth and feel the tears prick at my eyes, waiting for an answer that doesn't come.

"Did you know?" I look Harrison in the eyes, and he has the decency to look ashamed.

"We knew," he answers after a moment, and it's the last nail in the coffin. I lose all sense of composure.

"You didn't look for her? You didn't try to save her?" My breathing picks up, and I have to try hard to keep it steady.

"Petrov would've been a big fish to catch. The number of crimes and murders we could've stopped--" Harrison speaks calmly and with conviction, but that's not enough for me.

I cut him off and raise my voice as I ask, "One woman wasn't enough? How many women would have been worth it to step in?" Tears slip down my cheeks.

"We were keeping an eye on their location--" Carl starts to respond and I cut him off, too.

"Oh, so was she dead before, or after he shoved her in the trunk?" The room goes silent, and the only thing I can hear is the pounding of my heart in my chest.

"We did everything that we could--" Jerry starts to give me an excuse, but I'm not having it.

"Don't fucking lie to me." I'm so angry I'm shaking. I pound both of my fists on the table as my voice cracks. They knew, and did nothing. My heart beats too hard, my blood rushes too fast. "Why wasn't she good enough?" I feel my heart twist in my chest. Would Melissa have been good enough? Would they have saved her? Tears leak from my eyes as multiple people start talking over one another to justify their actions. This happens. Sacrifices are made. I know this. But it's not okay.

I stare into Harrison's eyes as I inform him, "She had a son." I don't bother wiping the tears off my face. I'm too far gone for this. "What if it had been your mother? Or your sister?" I yell out my questions so loud it makes my throat sore. I see Jerry reaching out for me from the corner of my eye. I stand up from the table and my chair falls back. I almost stumble over it, just trying to get out of the room.

She was a person. She was a victim. She was worth saving.

I would have saved her. I would have risked everything to save her.

"You don't understand. We couldn't risk the entire operation," Harrison calls out to me as I turn my back on him and leave. I can faintly hear the other officers, but I don't listen to what they're saying. I don't make it to my office. I turn the corner and crouch to the ground. Sobs tear through my chest and I know they can hear me, but I don't care. I have to purge this sickness that's taken over my body. I feel lightheaded and nauseated.

I would do anything to go back and save her.

I can't do this. I shake my head as my face heats and my hands tremble. It's too much. I've failed my sister, but I'm just not strong enough to handle this.

I brush away the tears with the back of my hand and slowly stand, resting against the wall.

I'll find another way. I can't chase ghosts anymore.

Chapter 20

Tonya

I look around my apartment, and it's almost pathetic how little there is to pack up. I don't know how I didn't notice. I look down at the open box next to my bookshelf. It's full of all my favorite romance novels. I used to love reading. From Fifty Shades and BB Hamel to Riley Rollins' Bad Boys and Marci Fawn's Mafia men. I huff a laugh, but it's humorless and pains my chest. I only read books with happily ever afters, but this is real life, and there's no guaranteed HEA for me.

I didn't take a single book out the entire time I've been here. I used to read every night. It's been so long. It was my stress relief. I could get lost in a book and forget the world around me. A woman with a book never goes to bed alone.

But I've been alone every night and I never sought out the comfort. I never tried to get lost in a different world. Maybe a part of me was just punishing myself, like I deserved to be alone and without any happiness.

I should call my mom to let her know I'm headed home, but I don't want to. The last time I called her she picked a fight. She likes to throw the fact that I used to party in my face. She likes to blame Melissa getting taken on me. She twists it around in such a sick way that I can see her logic. And I can't take that shit right now.

I pull my hair up and into a ponytail. It's just habit now. I hardly ever used to wear my hair up, but it's nice to get it away from my face. I'll have to think of something else though, I want as few reminders as possible. I want everything about these last few months to just disappear. It hurts too much.

I feel like a failure on so many levels. I know my sister wouldn't think that, or at least she wouldn't tell me that I failed her. My chest hurts just thinking about how she would try to console me if she knew how much I was hurting for her.

I'm not sure this pain will ever go away. I'm ready to deal with it, though. I have to. With no one to blame and no one to chase, all I have are memories flooding my thoughts. I lick my dry lips and take a seat on a box. I don't know what's in it, and I don't care. I just need to sit down. I've wasted too much time and energy searching for revenge. Harrison is right about one thing at least. There's always going to be someone like Petrov.

My heart pangs in my chest. I still don't know for sure. Tommy could've told me. I think if I'd asked him, he would've told me. I've thought that before though, and I was wrong. But something about our last time together makes me think...I close my eyes and stop that train of thought. I can't possibly think that.

Love isn't something I'm used to feeling. Not for a man. But the way he held me, the way he soothed every pain. My hands cover my face and I hunch over, sobs wracking my body. I'm such an idiot. What kind of person falls for a man like him? I'm a cop, for Chrissake! Or was a cop. I could've been killed. That's all I could think when I heard his brother's voice. They're going to kill us. The reality slapped me across the face.

But what if it was love?

The thought strikes my heart and causes a lump to grow in my throat. I try to stand, but a wave of lightheadedness and nausea make me slowly lower myself to the floor in a crouched stance. I balance myself on the balls of my feet for a moment. Once I think I can stand, I slowly rise, but the nausea hits again and I sprint to the bathroom.

I dry-heave into the toilet and it fucking hurts.

I turn and sit on the tiled floor with my back against the cabinet. My face feels hot and I close my eyes. I'm so tired and feel so sick. It's almost as if I'm pregnant.

My eyes pop open at the thought, and my heart refuses to beat in my chest. Pregnant. Fuck! I frantically try to remember the day. It's the end of the month. Fuck! Fuck!

I don't remember the last time I got my shot. I get one every three months. I've lost track of time, but I know I get them at the beginning of the month. I went a full month without birth control. How could I be so fucking stupid?

Fuck, no fucking way. I put my hand to my forehead as if I'd be able to tell I had a pregnancy temperature. Fuck! We've only been fooling around for a few weeks.

It only takes once.

Panic sets in and I storm through my apartment, picking up boxes until I get to a small one marked bathroom supplies. It was still half packed up until today, when I tossed the rest of the contents back in. I dig through it and find an old pregnancy test. The kind with a + sign for positive. It's not in a box so I look on the thick foil surrounding it for an expiration date, but I don't see one anywhere.

My skin heats and anxiety runs through me. I can't be pregnant. I can't.

I rip it open and leave the foil on the floor as I dart to the bathroom.

I've never been shy or anxious about peeing before, but it takes way too long for me to get a stream going, probably because I'm so nervous. Finally, my bodily functions obey and I put the stick under the stream for what seems like a long enough time and then slip the cap back on. I wipe it off with some toilet paper and set it down on the sink to wait, but I don't have to.

As the liquid runs through the window, I can already see it. Positive.

A faint + sign shows up almost immediately.

I stare at it without breathing.

I can't believe it. I'm pregnant.

Nausea and lightheadedness hit me at once, as if my body wants to confirm what the test is saying. I fall off the toilet and turn to hug the bowl as the sickness comes up. My skin flushes with heat, followed by chills as I wipe my mouth and try to sit up.

I'm pregnant.

I never planned for this. I never even considered children or a life where I settled down. I just didn't think it was for me. That kind of life was for my sister.

My hand hesitantly touches my belly, and tears well in my eyes. She would have loved to have a baby. But not with a man like Tommy.

I stand at the sink and turn on the water to gargle it and try to feel better.

I can't be far along. The thought enters my mind quickly, that I could leave and he'd never know. He'd most likely never find out. Even if he did, he's not the type of man who'd want a child. Right? If he found me, if he ever thought to look for me and found me with his child, I don't know what he'd do.

The thought makes my chest hurt even more. I'm bringing a child into this world and I don't even know if the man I think I love would want either of us.

I've felt strong my entire life. But right now, all I feel is weak.

I slowly stand and try to calm my breathing.

I can't just leave. I have to tell him.

If he doesn't want this baby, I'll leave and never come back. But if he does...I pause my steps and lean against the wall. If he does, I don't know what I'll do. I can't stay. I doubt he'd ever leave his *familia*. As if they'd give him a choice. I close my eyes and shake my head as I walk to the bed, gripping the locket in my hand. I lie back and try to think of what my sister would do. I know what she'd do. She'd tell him she was pregnant. And she'd move on with her life, loving her child. She may have never seen herself as strong. But she was. She was so fucking strong for always doing the right thing and sticking to what she believed in.

"I need you." My fingers slowly scroll over the locket's tiny engravings. "I need you right now." I whisper my words in a pained voice as tears slowly roll down my cheeks.

Do the right thing. That's what she'd tell me. She'd smile. She'd make sure this baby was born into a life surrounded by nothing but love.

And I will, too. I won't settle for anything else. I wipe the tears away and get my shit together. I breathe in with a long inhalation, and breathe out just as long.

Holy fuck, I'm really pregnant. An hour ago I felt like I had nothing, and no one. And now, everything has changed.

Chapter 21

Tonya

The walk up to Tommy's apartment is difficult. Every step toward him brings me closer to knowing whether or not he'll want me and this baby. My hand settles on my tummy as I get to the first landing and continue walking up the stairs. The outcome is most likely going to kill a piece of my soul. He can't be with me, and a man like him doesn't want to settle down with a baby. But it's the right thing to tell him. So I have to do this.

With my resolve firm, I brace myself to walk up to his door, but when I look up, my heart freezes in my chest. Vincent Valetti stares back at me with a look of contempt.

I push down all the emotions I'm feeling and school my

face. My heart pounds in my chest with fear. I can't die now. Now when I have this life to protect.

"Officer Kelly." Vince speaks with a hard voice and an even harder expression.

"Miss Kelly, now," I respond without backing down from his stare. He may be the Don, and he can definitely hurt me, but I know better than to show weakness to men like him.

"Oh, I see. Did you think that'd make it alright for you to cuddle up to my men?" he asks.

The way he says it makes me want to knee this prick in his groin. I may not be in a committed relationship, but I'm not a whore. And what he's implying pisses me off.

"No, I didn't. And if my slut memory is correct, I've only been fucking Tommy, so you can shove that bullshit right back up your ass."

He narrows his eyes and grinds his teeth. He's looking at me like he's not sure what to do with me. After a long moment of neither of us backing down he says, "I didn't mean to offend you."

"Yes you did," I'm quick to answer.

He grins at me with a twinkle of delight in his eyes and agrees, "You're right. But I'm generally not fond of cops. Please accept my apology."

My eyes finally break away from his and I feel like I can breathe. I nod and swallow thickly, looking at Tommy's door.

"You're here to see Tommy, then? You quit to be with

him?" he asks.

I shake my head. "No, I quit because I never should have been a cop."

"You don't think you have what it takes?" he assumes.

"No, I think I'd be a great cop if I had the determination for it. If I had the heart for it. But I don't. I joined for the wrong reason."

"What reason is that?" He tilts his head as if he's sizing me up. He's going to judge me, just like everyone else. I don't give a fuck, though. They can all judge me if they like, but I'm not going to change for them.

"Because my sister was taken by Petrov. I wanted to find him; I wanted to kill him."

"So you wanted to know about Petrov?" he asks, and I know exactly what he's thinking. He thinks I was trying to get information out of Tommy. He thinks that's why I was with him. That may have been the reason in the beginning, but that's not why I slept with him. And I hate that Vincent thinks that.

"Yeah," I answer him, not willing to elaborate.

"And now you've quit?"

"Yes." He looks at Tommy's door with a pissed-off look. He thinks Tommy told me. I can't let him think that. I don't want Tommy to get shit for it, and I won't have to lie anyway.

"He never told me. Even after we were together and everything happened between us. He never told me, but I think he's dead." *Between us.* My walls go down and I have to work real fucking hard not to break down. Maybe it was one-sided, and I just imagined him feeling anything toward me.

"So you *think* he's dead, so you quit." Although it's not a question, I know he's asking.

"No. I've had a hunch he's been dead for awhile now. I quit because I realized revenge wasn't the answer. There's always going to be someone to fight. I'm not the person to do it. I need to find another way."

"Another way to do what?" he asks.

"To let go." Tears prick at my eyes and I feel so fucking weak. I try to keep my composure and walk closer to Tommy's door. "I just need to tell him something."

"What do you have to tell him? I'd be happy to relay the message." He takes a step closer to me, and I instantly take a step back. I don't feel the same sense of security with him as I do with Tommy. I don't think I've ever felt that way about anyone before.

"Tell me," he says, but I can't.

"I--I can't." I've never spoken to Vincent Valetti before today. And I have no idea what kind of man he is, or what all he knows about us.

"Is it about police matters, or personal?" he asks.

I stare at the door, not knowing how to answer that. I don't want Tommy to get hurt.

"That's what I thought. You know that's not smart, right?

A cop, and a man like Tommy?" He shakes his head before continuing. "It's over now, isn't it?"

"I came to tell him something before I leave." A part of me just wants to tell Vincent so I can leave and avoid the rejection I feel coming.

"Good. It's a good thing you're leaving. It's for the best."

I look back at him, not sure how to respond. It fucking hurts. All of this is really none of his goddamn business.

He presses his lips into a straight line and then he asks, "You tell anyone about this little arrangement you had with Tommy?"

"No. It's over, so it doesn't matter." The words come out hard, but I stand my ground and maintain eye contact.

Vince rocks on his heels and looks to the left. "Good. So what do you have to tell him?"

"Something that's none of your concern." He narrows his eyes, but I don't care.

"Tommy's in a bit of hot water right now, sweetie, so you might want to be a little bit more forthcoming." The way he says it makes my heart stop. I don't want Tommy to get hurt because of me. My mother's words ring in my head, *it's all because of you.*

"I'm pregnant." The words fall from my mouth, and his eyes widen in surprise as he looks at my stomach. I feel the need to explain, so I blurt out, "It's early. I can't be any more than a few weeks along."

"So it's been going on for a few weeks, huh?" he asks.

"About that, yeah." I answer him and he nods his head. His eyes stay pinned on me, like he can read my thoughts. He's judging me. And along with me, Tommy.

"Are you sure it's his?" he asks me with an odd expression.

"I don't fuck around." I bite out the words with a little anger and instantly regret it. He hardens his expression and stares back at me. "Yes," I say.

"Why?" he asks me, without any indication of what he's referring to.

"Why what?" I look at him with confusion. Surely he isn't expecting me to tell him why women get pregnant. In my case it's because I'm a fucking idiot who got lost in a man's touch and wasn't thinking straight.

"Why'd you go after him?" he asks me.

"I didn't. It just happened. We didn't mean for this to happen." It strikes me that Tommy may be in deep shit. Really deep shit. "He tried to end it, more than once." I breathe in deep, remembering how he left me, how he never showed and sent me a text. Each time he tried to break things off I knew it was for the best, but it still hurt.

His brows raise in humor. "So he was that good, huh?" He huffs a small laugh and I give him a sad smile in return. That's all I can offer.

Vince puts a hand on my back and hesitantly gives me a pat as he says, "It'll be alright. I'll have him call you." His comfort is awkward, like he doesn't want me to cry, but he doesn't know what to do to make me stop.

"He's gonna be okay, right?" I ask him, before turning to walk away.

His eyes narrow, and I shake my head and wish I hadn't said anything. "I shouldn't ask questions. I take it back." He looks at me for a long time and I just want to hide.

"My wife didn't learn as fast as you. She's got a real problem with being nosy."

I look at him with a bit of worry.

"You know she tried to kill me once?" My mouth falls open in a little shock and I'm not sure what to say. "It was a horrible effort, really. But I'm just saying, shit can start out rough and end up alright."

I stare back at him, speechless.

He smiles at me as he says, "Everything's gonna be alright. I trust you'll see that soon."

Chapter 22

Tonya

I'm still shaken up as I park my car. It's different to say I'm pregnant out loud. It makes me feel more vulnerable than I ever have before. It almost hurts, admitting the insecurity that I may be on my own and Tommy may truly want nothing to do with either myself or our baby. I take a look at my apartment building and I have to squint. Something's different. My heart pounds in my chest. The light, it's too dark. My breathing halts as I realize the street light is broken. Something's wrong. No, I'm just freaking out. It's okay. It's just a light. I tell myself that over and over as my eyes dart from my left to my right.

Something deep in my chest is telling me something is

wrong. Something is not right.

I'm not safe. I hear my sister's voice screaming at me to run. *"Run!"*

Warning bells ring in my ears and I quickly turn the key in the ignition. But it's too late.

The window smashes and something hard crashes into my skull, splitting the skin on my forehead. I scream out and try to put the car into drive, but large hands reach in and grab my body. Blood drips down my face as strong hands wrap around my neck. I try to scream; I try to fight. The seat belt digs into my skin and holds me down as I hear the doors being unlocked. I open my eyes and see a large man wearing all black open the passenger side door and reach across the console. He's older, and his skin is tanned and wrinkled. His lips are thin and his eyes are deep set and dark. I try to move and get away, but I'm pinned in place by the man I can't see reaching in through the window.

The man to my right turns off the car and removes the keys. I feel hopeless and weak. I should've known better. How could I let this happen? Anxiety courses through me.

"You will not scream." The man in the passenger seat speaks in a deep, low voice. A voice I don't recognize. Maybe Vincent didn't trust me after all. Maybe they've come to kill me because of Tommy. My heart twists with agonizing pain. Maybe they killed Tommy. It's also possible that Tommy knows. My throat dries up as the man slaps his hand across my face. The slap burns my skin, and it's so forceful that it splits my lip.

"You will answer me!" I hear a faint accent as he yells at me. Russian. My eyes pop open and I stare back at the man.

His lip curls into a sick smirk. "Do you recognize me, Officer Kelly? You should. We know who you are." I do. I've seen his face before. He's a member of the Russian Bratva not far from here. One of the last times Petrov was seen was on their territory.

Revenge. They're here for revenge. But we didn't kill Petrov.

My eyes widen with fear. *Maybe he's still alive.*

A sick part of me wishes it were true. I find strength in thinking I'll see him. I want to see his face. My fear and anguish dissolve into nothing but sheer determination.

The hand over my mouth slowly moves away. I wish I could wipe the spit off of my mouth, but I can't. The arm pinning me down doesn't move.

"You're going to listen to me, and answer me when I tell you to." I stare back at the man who thinks he's calling the shots.

"Yes," I say obediently. I'm just waiting for my chance.

"You're going to call Tommy," the man says, staring me in the eyes. "We need one Valetti. And he'll come to you any time you call him. He doesn't tell anyone, just sneaks off to find his bitch in heat."

"Why?" I ask him in a calm voice. So calm it nearly terrifies me. I don't recognize my own voice.

"Why do you think, sweetheart?" He gives me a twisted

smile. "We need to set an example." He looks at the man holding me and I'm released. I hear more glass fall as the man to my left leaves my side and opens my door. "Be a good girl, and call him."

I look down at my purse and consider doing just that. But I don't want to lead him to his death. "Don't you want to live?" he asks. If I didn't know I was pregnant, I would never do it. But I have to do what I can to save my baby.

They'll never let you live, a sad voice whispers in my ear. My eyes dart to his. They're dark and full of excitement. I know they're going to kill me. There's nothing I can do to stop them. I turn my head, and see there are two more men standing outside the car. Four men total.

I think back to the alley. There were only three, and I had my gun in my hand aimed at one. I had an advantage there, that I don't, here. My heart stutters in my chest. I'm not going to be okay. I can't do this. And I need to. I can't fail.

I look back at the man as I take out my phone. I have to call Tommy. He's my only hope.

Chapter 23

Tommy

I've never been nervous going into Vince's house, never. It's a good sign that Elle opened the door and didn't seem to act any differently. It's funny seeing her with a baby in her arms. She's carrying him around like a pro now.

I open the door and reluctantly take a seat across from Vince. I know this isn't good. All his text said was that we needed to talk. I wonder what happened between Sunday and now. A million possibilities are running through my head. I don't think he'd kill me, not his own blood. Especially not with Elle around. But giving me a head start to run, or telling me to go away and never come back? That thought is a very real possibility.

I don't know how I ever thought I could get away with being with Tonya. I never should've fucked with a cop. I swallow and it hurts my dry throat. I crack my knuckles and try to relax, but I can't. If I had to take it back, I don't think I would. That's the worst part of it all. There was something between us that I'm glad I felt. Even if it left a scar on my heart. I wouldn't change it.

They may think it was wrong. But there was nothing wrong about what we did.

"We gotta talk, Tommy," Vince says from across his desk. His body is stiff. It's not a good sign. As I open my mouth, my phone goes off. Vince's eyes dart to my pants.

I should've put that shit on silent. I take it out quickly to turn it off and see it's Tonya that's calling. My bad girl. She sure has some real shit timing. I don't know why she's calling me. She shouldn't be. She should know I can't answer. I look Vincent in the eyes and I know that he knows who's calling. I hit the switch to turn it to vibrate and put it on his desk.

The shit part is that I would've answered her. Even though we've said our goodbyes. If I was anywhere other than here, I would've answered.

"You need to make a decision today, Tommy. If you go to her, you're leaving the family," Vince says simply. It fucking hurts. He's telling me he'd kick me out. My own blood. The *familia* is all I know. They're all I have.

"It's like that?" I ask him, not holding back how hurt I am.

Fuck it, he should know what he's asking.

"We can't have a cop in our family." I bite the inside of my cheek, letting the pain consume me. My eyes settle on a dark swirl in the rug beneath my feet. "It's over. I told you that." My voice is flat, just like my emotions.

"I know you did. But you have to have one more talk with her." My eyes dart to his. What the fuck does he want from me? I'm not using her. She's staying out of whatever shit he's thinking up in his head.

"She's leaving town. She quit being a cop, did you know that?"

She quit? Damn. I wish I knew why. My brow furrows. I don't know why it hurts me to think that she quit. I should be happy. That means she's not a cop anymore. But whatever her reason is for quitting must have something to do with how fucked up she was the other night. And I don't like that. I don't want anything to hurt my bad girl. And something did, something tore her up. And I'm not there for her. She needed me. She still does. I know she does.

"No, I didn't know." She never told me, maybe that's why she called. Just as I think that, the phone goes off again. It's a gentle vibration. The screen lights up and I see her number.

We both ignore it.

"She went to your place today."

My heart stops in my chest and I lean forward in my seat. I have to grab the armrests so hard my knuckles turn white just to stay seated. "You better not have fucking touched her." I swear to God if he laid a hand on her I'll fucking kill him.

He cocks a brow at me and shows no signs of fear. That's why he's the Don, but I know my threat didn't fall on deaf ears.

"She came to tell you she's pregnant."

His words strike me with a force that makes me fall back in the chair. I stare at the phone as the words settle. She's pregnant. She's going to have my baby.

"So you need to choose between her or the family, Tommy." Vince's words smack me across the face and bring me back to reality.

"Choose? Between family and my child? I fucking love her, Vince. I'm not giving her up." Saying it out loud feels so fucking good. I love her. And I love that she's having my baby.

"I'm sad to see you go, then." He's firm in his response.

"You said she quit." He can't honestly expect that I'm going to leave her when she's pregnant.

"I can't allow it, Tommy. Do you know what kind of position this puts me in?" My anger comes back with full force, just as the phone rings, *again*.

"Fucking answer it already." He looks at me with an exasperated expression. It pisses me off, but I answer it.

"Hello," I answer her without giving anything away.

"Thomas," she answers me with my name like that, and I hate it. Just because we ended things doesn't mean that she's gotta do that shit. I loved hearing her call me Tommy.

"Talk to me, baby." I hope my answer warms her up to me. I know she's gonna tell me she's pregnant and she's probably worried. I don't want her to be though. I'm gonna be there for her. Even if Vince tells me I've gotta leave, I'm not leaving her.

"I need you to meet me," she says calmly. There's no emotion from her at all.

"Sure, baby. Wherever you want." Again I soften my voice. I want her to know I'm receptive to whatever it is she's gotta tell me. I'm also anxious though. I wanna hear it from her lips. "We could talk now, if there's something on your mind," I offer.

"It's nothing." My forehead creases. Nothing? She's carrying my child, and she thinks it's nothing?

"I just want to see you before I leave. I thought we could meet where we first met. A small smile plays at my lips as I answer her, "At the station." She doesn't laugh. Instead she replies flatly, "At Rosetti's. I know it's closed now, but it'd be nice to say goodbye by the creek in the back. Where we first met."

Something's off. My eyes bore into Vince's skull until he looks at me.

"Something's wrong." I mouth the words to him as I put it on speaker. We've never been there before. It doesn't make sense. She's trying to tell me something. "Sure, baby, you want me to bring anything?"

"No, I think it will be quick." I don't understand what she's getting at, what she's hinting at.

"Maybe a bottle of wine. I can bring those chocolates; you remember the two packages we had at your place the first night? The two on the end table before I had your taste on my mouth for the first time. How many of those are you expecting?" I'm hoping she's getting what I'm talking about. Vince looks at me like I've lost my damn mind.

"I think four would be good." She's quick to answer, and I nod my head. Four men. I knew it. Thank fuck my girl is so smart and so damn strong.

"Alright, baby. What time do you need me there?" I ask.

"As soon as you can." Her last word comes out with strain. My heart aches in my chest like it never has before.

"Hey, baby, you okay?" I have to ask, even though I know she's not.

"I'll be better when you get here." With those last words the phone cuts out.

I put the phone down and look at Vince, my cousin. The boss of my *familia*, but also my friend.

"What's wrong?" he asks as I try to compose myself. I can't help that I'm choked up. I just realized how much I love her. I just chose her over everything, and now she's in danger.

"There's gonna be shit happening tonight," I tell him. "I need you."

"You think it's a setup? She's setting you up?" Vince looks pissed.

"No. No, she wouldn't do that. But someone's got her,

Vince. Four men."

He stands up and runs his hand through his hair. "Fucking hell, Tommy." Vince looks out of the window like he's debating on what to do.

"You gonna leave me to go in there alone?" After everything we've been through, too. We grew up together. He's my blood. My *familia*.

He cusses under his breath. "You go in first, but we'll be there."

Chapter 24

Tonya

I can't stop my body from trembling. They didn't bother blindfolding me, but I'm gagged, and my wrists are tied behind my back and my ankles are bound. Zip ties dig into my skin. I'm on the ground, propped up against a shed to the right of the restaurant parking lot. There's a creek to my left, and I'm almost certain that's where I'll be soon. I guess they wanted to hit him with shock factor. His girl, tied up and gagged, in clear view of the dirt road that leads here. Just beyond the treeline is the highway. I can hear the cars. I can even see the headlights. But they can't see me. No one can save me.

Maybe Tommy, but I may have also led him to his death. I'm certain he knows this is an ambush, though. Why else would he talk in code? My heart stopped when he said packages. My eyes almost darted to look at the man holding the phone, almost gave me away. Thank fuck I stayed calm. Four men. The odds are against us, but hopefully with the warning I managed to give Tommy, he'll have a chance.

They dumped me here like I was a bag of trash. Tossed me to the ground and went to stand behind their cars. Two black cars blend into the dark. But they're there, and if he's looking for something off, he should see them. They aren't in their cars. They're standing behind the one closest to me, with their weapons drawn and ready.

Jagged rocks dig into my knees as I move slightly across the ground. I'm moving slowly, so they don't notice. They aren't paying attention to me. One's smoking, and the other three are talking in hushed whispers. I can barely hear though, except for the occasional laughs. They're also going back and forth between Russian and English, so even when I can hear them, I'm not exactly sure what they're saying.

I'm not certain, but I think they want him to watch me die. As soon as he drives down and sees me tied here and struggling, that's when they'll do it. Shoot me until I fall lifeless on the ground. Although one keeps saying how he wants to see Tommy run to me as they shoot us both. The others don't. They don't want to kill him right away. They have questions that need to be answered.

I don't care what they're saying. I know their endgame is

to have both of us dead. I'll most likely end up in the creek, and Tommy's corpse will be sent back as a message to the Valettis.

I'm not going to let either of those scenarios happen. I need to live; I have to survive this. And right now, there's only me. If I can get free, I can run. My eyes dart to the four men who are in plain view and holding guns. My heart beats rapidly in my chest. I'll have to wait until I have a chance, but I'll try. I can't fight back without having any weapons on me. That would be suicide. But I can give Tommy a warning, and I can run. That's my only hope.

There's a broken bottle only a foot from me. If I fall over, I should be able to snag a piece. There's only a single zip tie binding my wrists, and one more binding my ankles. I can do this. Ankles first, so I can run as soon as Tommy gets here.

I scoot my knees across the dirt and they scrape against the gravel. I ignore the pain. Just another inch and then I prepare myself for the fall. It's gonna fuck up my shoulder since I can't brace for it. But I can fucking take it. I crash against the ground and hit my shoulder. My head bounces from the impact. The men look over at me while I struggle to take a piece of glass in my hand. My fingers graze across a few small pieces, but they aren't large enough. The jagged chunks pierce through my shirt and cut into my skin. Again, it's not horrible, but fuck it hurts. The fucker smoking sets his eyes on me. He tosses his cigarette onto the dirt and walks over with quick strides.

His dark eyes stare into mine as my fingers finally find a large chunk. I'm quick to make a fist to conceal it, even though it digs into the palm of my hand. I can't risk him seeing it. It's my only chance at freeing myself.

My heart skips a beat as he grabs my shoulders and drags my body back to the shed. The glass and gravel scrape my legs and I try to cry out, but the gag mutes the screams.

"Stay!" he yells, pointing his finger at me like I'm a dog. It gets a laugh from the other men. His large hand grips my chin and then he smacks my face several times—not hard, just enough to demoralize me. "Bad bitch. Stay." His accent is thick. I rest my head against the shed and pretend that I've lost all hope. I let the tears that beg to be released, slide down my cheeks. He laughs sickly and his foul breath fills my lungs as he turns to leave me, walking back to stand with the others. They're talking louder now, and in Russian.

As soon as I hear them patting him on the back and laughing, I push the glass to the zip tie on my ankle. It almost slips from my hand. The blood from my hand makes it difficult to hold. But I keep my grip and move it back and forth across the plastic. The glass is uneven and cuts into my ankles a few times, but the pain doesn't register at all. My eyes are focused on the gap in the trees, marking the entrance to this area. Tommy will be here soon; all I need to do is free myself before that happens.

It feels like forever, but it must only be a few minutes until both the zip ties around my wrists and ankles have snapped. I don't move yet. My limbs are screaming at me to take off. But they don't need me alive, they just want to make it hurt that much more for Tommy. If I run, they could shoot to kill me and there's no reason they'd hold back. Even worse, if I did run and they caught me, I don't know what they'd do to me. But I'm sure they wouldn't let me get out again.

So I wait. My skin prickles with anxiety, and the only thing I can hear is my heart beating loudly in my ears. I remember my phone in my back pocket and I struggle to keep my movements slow. Every time one of them looks at me, I freeze and try to remain as still as possible.

I should call the cops. I need help, and I know they could possibly come in time to save me, but they may also find Tommy. I don't want him to get caught in the middle of this, but I have to do everything I can to save myself and our baby. My skin feels like ice as I dial the numbers 9-1-1 behind my back. But I've done it.

I can faintly hear the dispatcher speaking, even though I can't give her any verbal confirmation that I'm on the line. I hit a button every few seconds, hoping she'll catch on.

"Are you unable to speak?" I barely hear the words. I don't hit any keys.

"If you can hear me, dial a number." My thumb presses down. I barely hear a faint beep. I keep my eyes on my captors. They show no signs that they can hear anything.

"Assistance is on its way. Is there a threat in your immediate vicinity?" she asks.

The phone slips from my hand as I try to push a number. It falls to the ground with a faint thud. I watch them, but they don't hear it. I can't hear her anymore.

There's no one else.

All I can do now is wait. There's nothing else left that I can do to save myself. I need Tommy.

Chapter 25

Tonya

Time passes slowly, yet nothing happens. I keep my eyes on the road and then on the men. My heart won't calm, and my skin sweats with anxiety. He's coming. I know he is. But what if he isn't? What if the cops come and the men hear? It'll only take a single bullet to end my life before they take off.

I'm relying on someone else to save me. And I fucking hate that.

I think I hear a car coming through the trees and closer to the entrance, and it distracts me. It also gets the men's attention and they raise their guns. No, no! I can't let them shoot. I start to stand, but the deafening sounds of guns being fired stops me in my tracks.

Bullets ring out from my left and right. But I can't see

where they're coming from. They ricochet off the cars, and I instantly scramble back behind the shed to find cover.

I turn my body to run, but I slam into a hard, unmoving chest. My eyes flash to a set of light blue eyes, but before I can react, the man's pinning my arms down and carrying me toward the back of the shed. I kick out as hard as I can and land a blow to his shin. I try to push him off me as he curses and nearly drops me. I hear bullets hitting the metal of the cars. I hear men shouting and yelling. The sound of a man getting shot and falling to the ground fills my ears.

"Left, left!" someone calls out. These are the sounds of an ambush.

Fear overwhelms my body, but I force my limbs to push him away. I didn't come this close to escaping, just to be taken again. I refuse to stop fighting.

"Jesus, woman, I'm here to protect you." He pushes me against the shed with all of his body weight. I try to move my arm so I can get an uppercut in, but he leans his entire body against me, rendering both of us useless. I continue to struggle. I won't give up. "Calm the fuck down! Tommy sent me." My body stills as I hear a few men call out. "On the passenger side!" A bullet and then another.

"Tommy said stay here." He pulls away a bit. "He'll fucking kill me if you go out there."

I turn my head to face him as the sounds die down and see a kid. He can't be any more than in his early twenties. He's got shaggy hair and an uneven patch of stubble. He backs his body away slowly, looking at me like I might take off.

"Don't move," he says with his finger pointed at me. If I was in a different situation, I'd roll my eyes. But right now, I'm full of nerves and apprehension.

"Can I have a gun?" My body heats as I ask.

"Tommy said you'd ask for one." He laughs and slowly hands me a gun. The first thing I do is check for bullets. It's loaded. He eyes me warily. "You think he'd short you on ammo?"

"Not him, no," I say, taking a step toward the edge of the shed.

"Don't. He'll kill me. For real," he pleads with me, rocking on his feet. "Just stay here."

He takes a peek around the corner and grins. "They really only sent four." He shakes his head and smiles from ear to ear. "Fucking idiots." He turns to face me, leaving his body exposed, and I yank him back to the safety behind the shed.

"Take cover," I practically yell at him. Dumbass kid.

"They're done," he says defensively, with his forehead scrunched up.

"Stay back here until you hear otherwise." I feel like I'm back at the academy. This kid's gonna get his ass shot.

He smirks at me. "No wonder Tommy likes you." It's silent all around us; I think it's over. "You really a cop?" he asks.

Before I can reply, I hear the answer behind me.

"No, she's not." I turn and immediately wrap my arms around Tommy's neck. I have to stand on my tiptoes. His large arms wrap around my body as he lifts me up. He buries his head in my neck.

"Is it over?" I ask him, looking around to see something, anything, but I'm still in the back, so I can't see shit.

"It's over. Probably a little overkill," he says with a huff of a laugh.

"Really, only four?" the kid says from behind me. I lift my head up in Tommy's arms to face the shaggy kid.

"Well, they thought it'd just be me," Tommy explains.

"Dude, you should take offense to that."

"Get outta here, Brant." The kid takes off as Tommy turns me in his arms.

"Are you alright?" he asks me, as his eyes roam down every inch of exposed skin. He touches the small gash on my forehead and it makes me wince. "I'm so sorry, baby," he says in a voice so soft and sincere I can feel his agony.

I shake my head, "don't be. It's not your fault." He tries to object, but I give him a small kiss and try to distract him, but when I pull back there's still pain in his eyes.

He gently brushes the pieces of rock and glass off of me, but I fall against his chest and hold onto him. "It's alright baby, I'm right here." He pulls back from me and takes my chin in his hand. It feels so good to just be held by him. He gives me a soft, sweet kiss and it soothes every part of me. "Is the baby okay?" he asks, looking down on me with worry in his eyes.

Tears prick at my eyes as I say, "Vincent told you." My heart stops beating, and the world seems to blur around us.

"Yeah," he says, putting a hand on my belly as he asks, "Tell me you're alright?"

I push the words out through my sob, "I'm okay." I bury myself in his chest, feeling completely safe and secure. But then I remember, the cops will be here any minute. "You need to go. I called the cops."

At the word cops, the noise around us stops and I realize the other Valettis are still here.

"You called the cops?" Vince comes up to our left, and Tommy angles his body so that his shoulder is between me and Vincent. I hold onto him as my body heats and a wave of nausea hits me. I had to. I didn't know they were all coming. I never would've guessed that.

"What was she supposed to do, Vince?" Tommy asks. "We've got enough time to get out of here anyway."

Vince looks between the two of us and then says, "She has to stay here so they'll find her. Or else they'll come looking."

Tommy nods his head slowly, but he's clearly not planning on listening. His grip on me tightens. "Don't be stupid, Tommy. She'll be fine. She'll be out in a few hours," Vince points out.

"I don't wanna leave her." His words are absolute.

"I'll say I was inside the shed and I didn't see anything," I quickly say. Vince searches my face, like he's not sure if I'm being truthful or not.

"They touch you?" Vince asks. At first I'm confused, but then I realize what he's asking. I shake my head as my eyes fall and Tommy's grip tightens on me.

"You did real good. Guess they taught you something right, huh?" Vince talks to me, and I struggle to respond. I don't want to talk about being a cop with him. Not now, not ever.

I give him a tight smile in return and say, "Thanks."

"We saved your ass, remember that," he says before turning away from me. He yells out to the men who are picking up the bodies and lifting them into the back of their cars.

"I don't want to leave you," Tommy whispers into my ear.

"Go, baby, please." The danger is gone and the cops will be here soon. He needs to go. Him being here will only complicate things. It'll give the department leverage to use against the Valettis, and more ties to the Petrov case. The reminder of the case has me wanting to know if Petrov is truly dead. My eyes fly to Tommy's. I should ask him. I still don't know. The words are there, but I don't say them. The power they held before has waned. Before I can ask, I hear the sirens in the distance. "Go," I tell him, staring in his eyes, begging him to listen to me.

"I'll be watching and waiting, baby. I'll be right here for you." He kisses me again as Vince's car pulls up in front of us.

"Move your ass, Tommy! We gotta go!" he calls out, and I hear a door open.

"I love you, Tommy." I have to tell him. I can't hold it in anymore.

Before he leaves, he gives me a small smile and brushes the hair out of my face as he says, "I love you, too."

Chapter 26

Tonya

"You sure you didn't see anyone?" Jerry asks me, for the fourth time. He's nodding his head and trying to get me to talk. He should know I'm not going to say shit. I haven't for the last three hours. They found the blood at the scene. They ran tests and came back with nothing. All I told them was that I was taken against my will by men with Russian accents who wanted information.

I shake my head with downcast eyes. I hate lying and putting them in this position, but I'm not going to give them anything to lead them to the Valettis. I told them I was blindfolded the entire time. I hate lying, but I need to stick with the story.

The Russian mob is in deep shit, and there's plenty of

evidence on them. But nothing against Tommy or his *familia*.

"Not a damn thing that could tie them there?" Jerry asks. He has a hunch it was the Valettis who came in and took the Russians out. All three of us know it was them. It makes sense. A Russian mob on their turf? It doesn't take a genius to figure it out.

"You're fucking one of them, aren't you?" Harrison sneers at me from across the table. I fucking hate the way he says it. I also hate that he's right. He doesn't buy that I was taken in order to get information on the Valettis. That's the story I'm supposed to give the cops. That the Russians wanted intel on their routines and addresses. Everything and anything I knew about them. But it doesn't make sense that I would be left unharmed. Not unless the Valettis needed me alive. Or if I meant something to one of them.

Harrison can see right through that. I'm not a good liar. Jerry can as well, but he hasn't said anything. I can see the disappointment in his eyes.

"Get out, Harrison." Jerry doesn't yell, doesn't even turn to look at him.

Harrison clenches his fists and mutters an apology before stalking out of the room. There's no love lost between us. As the door closes, Jerry leans forward and asks in a low soothing voice, "Are you sure you're alright?" Concern is written all over his face.

"I'll be alright." I cross my arms over my chest and take a deep breath. I'm still a little shaken up. A lot shaken up maybe, but Tommy's there waiting for me. I close my eyes and I can feel his lips kissing my neck and his arms holding me close to him. He's my happy place. I need him, and now I have him. I'm not letting him go. I can't. He better know that.

"If you're in any trouble, you know to come to me. Don't you?" he asks, and I know he means it.

I nod my head. There may be times I don't agree with him, but I know he'd help me if he could. Right now I don't need help though. At least not from him.

"Are you sure you wanna go through with this?" He puts his hand on the table, offering it to me in a sweet gesture of comfort.

I accept and put my hand in his, and he squeezes. "I dug into you a bit after you left the conference room and found out about your sister. You may have joined for the wrong reasons, but you're a good cop. It's not too late to stay." He emphasizes the last line. If only he knew. It's too late for so many things.

"My mind's made up." I pull my hand away and breathe in deep.

"As long as you know what you're doing," he says, leaning back in his seat.

A short laugh erupts from my lips. "I have no clue what I'm doing," I confess. I run my hands through my hair and lean back, shaking my head. "I just want to be happy."

"You deserve to be happy, Tonya. Don't let him hurt you. And when the time comes, don't say I didn't warn you."

"He's not going to hurt me, not ever." I don't know when

the conversation changed, but we both know who we're talking about. I won't say it though. I won't name him.

"Not the way you're thinking." He walks to his door and locks it before shutting the shades. "What are you going to do when he gets charged with something, and it sticks?"

I shake my head, "I'll figure it out when it happens." My hand subconsciously goes to my belly. I jerk it away before he has time to see. I know he loves me; I know I love him. And he'll take care of us both.

"I hope he treats you right, Tonya. I really do. But if he ever does anything, or any of them ever do anything," he looks at me with absolute sincerity, "I'll be here for you."

"Thank you, Jerry."

"Don't thank me," he says bluntly. "You're asking for trouble." I know what he means, and I understand it, I really do. But I can't help what I want.

A sad smile plays at my lips as I say, "I'm good at that, apparently."

He looks at me for a long moment and I don't know what he wants from me.

"I'll be alright, Jerry. I promise you." I stand up and walk over to give him a quick hug.

He walks to the door and unlocks it, but before he opens it, he adds, "I just hate to see a good girl like you wind up with a man like him." I can't help the smile that grows on my face. He has no idea that I'm really a bad girl at heart.

Chapter 27

Tommy

That was intense. I'm shocked at how fucked up I am over that shit. I scouted it out first. It took everything in me not to run to her as that prick put his hands on her. I got that fucker. I took him down first. I've been in worse situations though. Vince brought everyone. It feels so fucking good to know he still had my back.

Those Russian pricks didn't stand a chance, and only two of 'em even got a shot off. They aimed at nothing. They couldn't see us in the dark. The one that took cover--fuck, if I was him, I would've just killed myself. Instead now he's sitting there, chained to a chair with a gag in his mouth. He should've known this was going to happen.

"Whatcha gonna do with him, boss?" I ask Vince.

"Well, we got the information we need, so I couldn't give two fucks. Figured you may wanna take some aggression out, since it was your girl he took." Vince walks over to the sink in the back room. We're in the basement of the safe house. It's fucking freezing down here. The fucker in the chair has bruises all over his face. His one eye is swollen so bad his face looks inhuman.

Anthony's drying off his tools. I instinctively look down and see three fingers on this fucker's right hand have been removed. That's usually Anthony's first move. They're easy to cut off, and it makes a pretty bold statement.

"So you got everything you need?" I ask Vince as he dries off his hands. He turns back to me.

"Yeah, they aren't going to fuck with us unless they want their entire operation shut down. Thanks, Nik!" Vince slaps a hand on the man's shoulder and he doesn't even react. He's so close to death.

"Alright, I'm good. Just kill the bastard," I say.

Vince looks at Anthony and he nods as we turn to leave. Anthony's not talkative when he's on the job. Never has been. I used to take offense to it. But now I get it; he has to be in the right headspace, and that doesn't include saying a fucking word.

"There's one more reason I called you down here," Vince says as we climb the stairs.

"I figured there was." And it's about Tonya. I know it is. I waited at the station and followed her home last night. I just held her all night; I needed to feel her. Knowing I almost lost her fucking hurts. I'm not letting her go. I can't.

"I understand that you wanna be with her. And truthfully, she's a nice broad." We walk into his kitchen and he grabs me a beer. The faint sounds of a chainsaw can be heard coming from the basement. It sends chills down my spine.

"I'm not leaving her, Vince. I can't do that." My stomach drops, knowing that what means. I don't wanna leave my family. The *familia* is all I know. But I'm not letting her go.

"I get that. I do." He passes a beer to me and shuts the fridge.

Leaning against the counter, he pops the cap off his beer with his keys. "She's still associated, Tommy." I put down my beer and shake my head as he tries to pass me his keys. I can't drink right now. "You know we can't have that shit."

"Yeah. I know." I do know. I wouldn't be a smart move to have that shit known.

"Good," he says with finality. "I'm sorry, Tommy."

I nod my head, my throat closes, and my heart tries to leap out of my chest. "What's it gonna mean, boss?"

"You can't do errands anymore. It can't happen. You can't represent the *familia*." I wanna argue with him, but I can't. I know it's true. Fuck--realistically, he should kill me. It's a risk keeping me alive. It's a risk letting her get close. "Not like that, anyway," he says, and it brings my attention back to him.

"I've been thinking about you and your brother. I think

it'd be good to finally take on those contracts. We'd get a shit-ton more money from the hits. And it'd keep us in a good place with our contacts. Anthony always said he'd need another person to help. That's what I want from you two, and he agreed already. Just need you in on this, too."

My heart slows, and I swear to God I lose feeling in my hands. "What do you mean?"

"I mean, if you're gonna be taking a cop as your girl, then you're going to have to be a contractor."

"A contractor?" I ask, not understanding.

"You two will do the hits. We'll give you the names and you get it done." I nod, taking it all in.

"What about the rest of the *familia* business?" I ask.

He shakes his head and says, "That's no longer a concern of yours. It keeps things a little neater."

"I understand." I take a moment to process it as he opens my beer himself and hands it to me. I finally ask, "Does that mean I don't have to call your ass 'boss' anymore?" We both give a small laugh. I have to admit it hurts a bit, but I understand. And I'm fucking grateful to still be around.

He smiles broadly. "It's the best I can do, Tommy. She's loyal to the family, and to you. That's enough for me. She's a good girl, like my Elle. She's not gonna say shit. So long as that's the case, everything's good."

"That mean I'm not made anymore?" That'd put some bigass targets on my back.

"You're still a Valetti. And just like last night, we've got you, and you've got us, right?"

I pull my cousin in for a hug and feel like a little bitch for getting even the least bit emotional. This is better than I'd hoped for.

"You'd better fucking marry that broad, too. The sooner, the better," he says.

"Yeah, I know, so she doesn't have to talk."

He looks back at me with a grin as he says, "Well, that and Ma will be pissed if you don't do right by her." His joke fills my chest with warmth. He's right, too. Aunt Linda will kick my ass.

"Love you, cuz," Vince says.

"Love you, Vince." We both pat each other on the back harder than we should to make up for getting so emotional.

"Still family?" I ask again, not really believing it could be that good.

Vince nods his head, "Always."

Chapter 28

Tonya

"You gotta meet the *familia*." Tommy wants to take me to his aunt's house for dinner. To Dante Valetti's house. Dante Valetti is the former Don and father of the current Don, Vincent Valetti. I'm nervous as hell. It's been two weeks of just us. Two weeks of hiding away in his apartment while we figure this shit out. There's no doubt in my mind that I made the right decision leaving the department and doing what feels right. But then I remember his family, and I'd be lying if I said I wasn't worried.

"They know I was a cop." That's the only explanation I need. That right there is enough for them to want me dead.

"Yeah, they do. And they know you're my girl." Tommy rubs his hand over my belly and forces a smile from me.

"You're a woman, Tonya, and I know you hate this, but we keep women out of it."

"But I was a cop." I've seen them all a handful of times now, and each time it gets easier. But this is different. It's not one or two of them coming over to drop something off, it's all of them in one place. And I feel like I'm going to be an outsider.

"Yeah, for under a year. And they know about your sister and why you joined. They know you're loyal to me." He stands behind me and wraps his arms around my body, pulling me into his hard chest. I feel cocooned in his warmth. I close my eyes and breathe in deep. It's not fair that he can put me at ease so effortlessly.

"Besides, there's someone there I really think you should meet."

"Who's that?" I ask.

"You should meet Ava. I think you'd really love getting to know her. She lost her sister, too."

"Ava?" The name rings a bell, but I'm not sure why.

"Yeah, she's been asking about you. She wants to meet you." He speaks his words softly, like he's waiting for something.

"Why does that name sound familiar?"

"Ivanov." He says her last name and everything clicks into place. I turn in his arms to face him with wide eyes. She's supposedly dead.

I part my lips, but I don't ask. I know not to ask questions.

He gives me a small smile and says softly, "A bad man hurt

her once, but she made him pay. She's a strong woman, like you. I think you two are going to get along great."

Tears prick at my eyes, and I hold onto him with everything in me. He kisses my hair, while I try to calm down.

"I'm sorry I didn't tell you sooner, but he's long gone, Tonya. He'll never hurt anyone else."

I cry in his arms. I haven't cried in weeks, but the need to purge all my sadness has me leaning against him in tears. He rubs my back while I cry for all of them. For my sister, for Ava's sister. For Ava and the other survivors. I cry for them all. A calmness washes through me as I settle with exhaustion into his embrace. A feeling like a rebirth. Like I'll finally have a fresh start. Maybe now I can finally get the catharsis I've been striving for all this time.

My blurry eyes catch a glimpse of the picture frame I put on Tommy's nightstand. It's the same picture that's in my locket. My hand reaches up and I grab onto it. We were just young girls in middle school and high school, but it's my favorite picture of us. I can't wait until we move and make a new place of our own. We need a fresh start. And moving is the way to make that happen.

I look up at Tommy with wonder, but also a sense of insecurity. I haven't forgotten what Jerry said, and if I'm honest with myself, I'm worried about Tommy and about him staying in the *familia*.

"Spit it out, baby." His hand settles on the nape of my

neck, and his thumb brushes along my jaw. It soothes me. Everything about him soothes me.

"I don't know if I can live with you doing this, Tommy. I don't--" I just want to list all the reasons this is so wrong. But his lips silence mine in a sweet kiss.

I moan into his mouth, just loving his touch. He pulls back, and looks at me with sincerity.

"I told you, I'm not working for the *familia* anymore." I know what he said, but he's too fucking happy for that to really be the case.

"Forget about right and wrong for just a moment. Just listen to your heart, baby. What does it want? Us being together may be fucked up and wrong. But it's what I want."

I struggle to respond. He's right. I do want him. He's the only thing I want.

"Just give me a chance to love you." His hand brushes along my belly, where our baby's growing.

It may be wrong, but I want him. I love him.

He must see that I've decided. He smirks and says in a playful tone, "You know you're my bad girl."

I shake my head and let a small laugh escape me. Tommy takes my chin in his hand and kisses me. My lips mold to his and I give in.

I love him, and that's all that matters.

"I love you, Tommy," I whisper as he pulls away from me.

"I love you, too."

Epilogue

Tommy

I'm so fucking nervous. I don't remember the last time my heart beat so damn hard in my chest. I shake out my hands again and start pacing.

"I'm telling you, she's gonna say no." I turn on my heels to face Anthony. The fucker's grinning from ear to ear.

"You fucking love this, don't you?" I ask him.

He smirks back at me and says, "You know I do. You get all stressed out about shit you shouldn't be worried about." He takes a sip of his drink and then adds, "Besides, you'll have plenty of stress when the next list comes in."

He's right. I'm not as calm as Anthony is yet. I'm doing hits with him now. I'm cut off from *familia* business, and taking the contract hits instead. Anthony's been showing me the ropes. And I have to admit I'm enjoying it, but I've got a ton of shit to learn.

I should probably be worried that I'm not really seen as a member of the *familia* by outsiders, but I'm not. Vince told me not to be. He's my cousin, my blood, and he's grown to love Tonya. All the family has.

He said things need to blow over, time to settle down. And I'm fine with that. I'd be lying if I said I was unhappy taking these hits with Anthony. It's a nice change of pace, and less risk than what I'm used to. I don't really give a shit what I do, so long as I have my family and my girl.

She's accepted, especially with the women. They've been pampering the hell out of her since she's pregnant with our little boy. She's having a difficult time now that she's so far along. But he's going to be here soon. We can't fucking wait.

"You're thinking about him, aren't you?" Anthony asks. Then he teases, "He's gonna ruin your sex life."

I shake my head and grin at him. He's got a shit-eating grin on his face. "You said her pregnancy was gonna ruin our sex life, and look how good that turned out." I can hardly keep up with her. My bad girl still wants me. All fucking day if she can. "You're so damn negative, you know that?" I tell him, as I peek out of the back doors and into the restaurant.

"Yeah, I'm a little jealous, I gotta admit that."

I look at my brother with surprise. "Of me?" He's never

been jealous of me my whole life.

He scrunches his forehead as he replies, "Don't look at me like that. I can be jealous if I want."

"If you wanna girl, go get one. You wanna baby, go make one."

He huffs a laugh and downs his drink. "It's not quite that simple, Tommy."

I start to tell him, "Yeah, it is that simple," but think back and realize that no, it's not. Not for the right one. Then I hear my girl. She's laughing, and I'd recognize that beautiful sound anywhere. I open the door a crack and look out.

She's in black leggings and a hot pink sweater that hugs her swollen belly. She went out for ladies' night and looks so damn happy. Ava's hanging on her arm. The two of them are close now. Thick as thieves. I've gotten to know more about Kane than I ever wanted.

"Showtime." Anthony smacks my shoulder and gets ready to open the door.

"Not yet." I say quickly, shutting it and taking a deep breath.

"Bro, knock it off. It's in the bag." I look back at him and try to calm my nerves. "For real, Tommy. She loves you." He pats my back and adds, "She's gonna make a good wife."

I nod my head. She is. She's gonna be my wife. And I'm going to give her our happily ever after that she deserves.

Anthony smiles at me. "That's the Tommy I know. Go get yourself a wife." He opens the door and I take a few steps out into the restaurant.

She's facing away from me in her seat. They sat her like that on purpose. Ava sees me first, and lights up. She grabs a drink menu and tries to distract Tonya. The ladies look up at me one by one, and try to not make it obvious.

Aunt Linda's smile is so fucking big, though. She's gonna give it away. She covers her face with her hand and pretends to cough. I get down on my knee behind her and look to my right to see the guys coming out. We're all ready to surprise her with a baby shower. I knew I wanted to do this in front of everyone, and doing it here and now, it just felt right.

While the ladies distract her, the guys open up the back room doors where the party will be. I hear them all standing behind me. It's go time. I know it is, but I can't fucking move. My nerves are getting the best of me.

I shake out my hands with my eyes closed, and that's when I hear her.

"Tommy?" Her voice is full of shock. I open my eyes with the ring box in my left hand, get down on one knee, and see her wide-eyed and covering her mouth. She's got her hands up like she's saying a prayer.

"You're such a bad girl. You were supposed to wait till I told you to turn around." I smirk at her. Just seeing her excitement and the happiness in her eyes puts me at ease.

Her hands fly down and start flapping like she's a little kid.

"Tonya Ann Kelly, marry me." I hold up the box to show

her the three carat, cushion cut diamond ring with side accents I've picked out for her. I went to three different stores, but the second I saw this one, it was all over. I knew I needed to put this one on her finger.

She flings herself at me and wraps her arms around me. I don't wait for her to answer. I slip the ring on her finger, where it belongs. Everyone's clapping and laughing. I can hear Aunt Linda crying, 'cause that's what she does. But the best sound is coming from my bad girl's lips. She's got her head buried in my neck while she clings to me, "I love you so much Tommy. I love you."

I pull back to look into her gorgeous eyes; they're full of nothing but happiness. "I know you do, baby. I love you, too."

About the Author

Thank you so much for reading my romances. I'm just a stay at home Mom and an avid reader turned Author and I couldn't be happier.

I hope you love my books as much as I do!

More by Willow Winters
www.willowwinterswrites.com/books

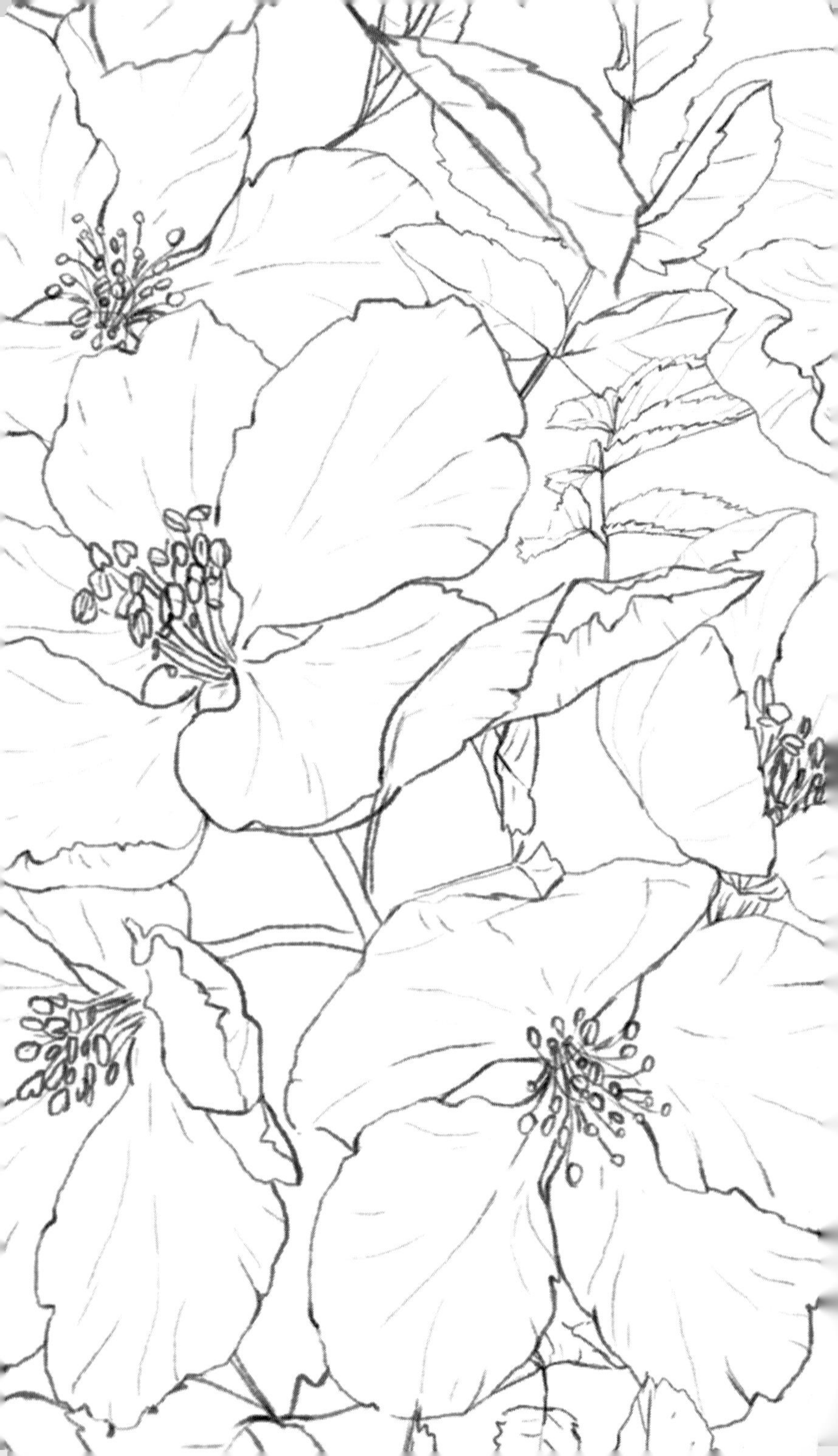

Printed in Great Britain
by Amazon